P9-DMK-346

HARRY and Augusta were alone and Augusta felt panic, wondering how she could continue this charade. As he advanced towards her, Augusta could feel the trembling begin in her knees and hands and could do nothing to stop it.

"Why, what is this, Sophia?" he asked. "Your hands are trembling."

He tilted her chin with his finger so that she was forced to look at him, and very gently and softly kissed her lips. She felt herself melting and without conscious volition kissed him back. His arms went about her and pulled her close and for one passionate moment they were entirely lost. Then she realized she was kissing her sister's betrothed and pushed him away violently. They stood staring at one another in confusion until she fled.

Harry watched her go, his mind filled with a jumble of flashing, disconnected thoughts. Then suddenly he said aloud, "That was Augusta!"

Fawcett Crest Books
by Norma Lee Clark:

MALLORY

SOPHIA AND AUGUSTA

UNABLE TO FIND FAWCETT PAPERBACKS AT
YOUR LOCAL BOOKSTORE OR NEWSSTAND?

If you are unable to locate a book published by Fawcett, or, if you wish to see a
list of all available Fawcett Crest, Gold Medal and Popular Library titles, write
for our FREE Order Form. Just send us your name and address and 35¢ to help
defray postage and handling costs. Mail to:

FAWCETT BOOKS GROUP
P.O. Box C730
524 Myrtle Ave.
Pratt Station, Brooklyn, N.Y. 11205

(Orders for less than 5 books must include 75¢ for the first book and 25¢ for
each additional book to cover postage and handling.)

SOPHIA AND AUGUSTA

Norma Lee Clark

FAWCETT CREST • NEW YORK

To
DIMITRI

Σαγαπό

SOPHIA AND AUGUSTA

Published by Fawcett Crest Books, a unit of CBS Publications
the Consumer Publishing Division of CBS Inc.

Copyright © 1979 by Norma Lee Clark
ALL RIGHTS RESERVED

ISBN: 0-449-23916-0

All the characters in this book are fictitious, and any resemblance
to actual persons living or dead is purely coincidental.

Printed in the United States of America

10 9 8 7 6 5 4 3 2 1

Chapter One

Mrs. Charles Portman sat cozily before the fire in her drawing room, deep into a letter from her mother. Since her mother had a great deal to tell her, the older woman had crossed her lines more than once, which made the decipherment of her writing a little difficult.

Her mother's report on the state of things at Linbury seemed to indicate that all was well there, and the rest of the letter dealt with gossip about their neighbors, and the activities of her younger daughter, Caro, who was very happy with the mare that dear Charles had sent to her, and thanked him very much for his kindness. Mrs. Tolgarth rhapsodized for several lines about her good fortune in having such a son-in-law as dear Charles, with which statements his wife was in entire agreement, as could be seen by the smug smile on her lips as she read. Her mother ended with the request that Mallory give her best love to dear Augusta and dear Sophia, and much to her own darling daughter, Mallory.

Mallory Portman let the letter drop into her lap and sat staring into the fire, pictures of Linbury rising seductively in her mind. She missed Linbury very much now that spring was nearly upon them, and even more, she missed her dear friends there: comfortable Mrs. Quinn and her two madcap daughters, the Fordyces, and even dear old Lady Armstead. Mallory wondered how soon they could expect Lady Armstead's son, Courtley, to follow them up to London. He had been dangling after Sophia for ages now, even before Mallory had met the twins.

However, Mallory thought, as she held her toes closer to the lovely fire, she was not discontented to be here. This was her second Season with the twins in London, and the difficult part was finished with. They had been presented at Court, made their first entrance at Almack's, been an instant success, and were to be seen everywhere last autumn. After a lovely retreat at Linbury over Christmas, the twins were now eager to renew their acquaintance with their London friends and enter the social whirl again.

Mallory had fallen in love with the Portman townhouse on first sight, and the staff were all wonderful, so the family members were quite as comfortable here as in the country, even though the air was not as fresh, and there were no lovely walks and rides through the woods. On the other hand, Mallory had been met with much warmth and many good wishes from her old acquaintances of her own Season in London, when she had been eighteen. Everyone had been so genuinely happy for her, in her good fortune to marry the wealthy and handsome Charles Portman. And now the bliss of her secret joy, the one she carried within and hadn't shared with anyone yet, not even Charles—so new it was, this tiny seed beginning to blossom. *My little boy,* she thought happily. *Or my own baby girl, with Charles' brown eyes and dimples.* Dreaming sweetly in this way, she drifted comfortably to sleep.

In her sleep it seemed that a butterfly was tickling first her nose, then her eyelids, and then her lips. She slowly opened her eyes to find her husband bending over her, kissing each of those places lightly.

"Oh, darling Charles, how nice," she said sleepily, smiling up at him.

"And what is this, nodding off by the fire in the middle of the day like an old lady? I'll have to get you a cap," he teased, pulling up a stool and sitting at her knee.

"Just contentment, my love. And perhaps something else," she added mischievously.

"Ah, dreaming of a lover, that must be it. Who have you captured this time. Is that silly Beaumont boy still dangling about?"

She giggled, "I know it is dreadful of me to laugh, but he is the silliest thing imaginable, Charles. He wrote me a poem yesterday, all moonlight and dew on rose petals. It was all I could do to keep a straight face. Are you sure it's the fashionable thing for married women to allow unattached young men to be forever hanging about one?"

"All the crack," he asserted firmly.

"But are you not jealous?" she asked curiously.

"What? Of that young puppy? What do you take me for? It will be a fine day when I become jealous of that willowy, green tadpole!"

She laughed again. "Very sure of yourself, aren't you?"

"Very," he said simply, and pulled her forward to kiss her soundly.

She leaned back finally, with a sigh of contentment, and they sat for a while in silence. He put his head down on her knee and she slowly and sensuously ran her hands through his hair, and gradually the small, smug smile reappeared. He raised his head suddenly and surprised her with the smile still on her face.

"Aha! I knew it! The 'something else' you mentioned before."

"What do you mean?" she asked innocently.

"Don't haver with me, my girl. Before, you said about contentment and perhaps something else. I've not forgotten, and now I want an explanation. What else?"

"Well, we are to have someone joining us, you see, and I'm quite looking forward to it."

"Your mother and Caro coming up from Linbury?"

"No. It's no one you've met before, nor have I, come to that."

"Well, then, how can you be so pleased? Mallory, you are teasing me and you know what the family punishment is for teasing," he threatened.

"No, no, Charles, do not tickle me. I will tell you. This guest will not be coming until—let me see—about next Christmas I would say."

"What! Eight months from now? Well, I fail to see how you can be excited by someone who won't be arriving till—" He stopped suddenly, looked at her to find her smiling broadly at him and nodding.

"Mallory! Do you mean—oh my darling, *darling* Mallory." And with that he lifted her and sat down with her in his lap and kissed her, lingeringly this time.

The sounds of the London streets faded away and the room was possessed by quiet murmurings of love and happiness and the crackling of the fire.

The door opened abruptly to admit two young ladies, who bore not just an amazing resemblance to each other, but were, unbelievably, exact duplicates.

"Oh, for heaven's sakes, they're noodling again. Is that all you two can ever think of?" said Augusta with pretended exasperation.

"Darling Mallory, we're so sorry to burst in on you like this," said Sophia.

"And so you should be," said Charles crossly. "It seems to me the two of you wait to be sure you will be interrupting something before you pounce."

Mallory hastily disentangled herself from Charles' arms and rose. "Nonsense, Charles. Sophia, close the door and do you both come in and be comfortable. Isn't the fire nice on this gray day?"

"Oooh, it's lovely, Mallory. We just came back from the Tilburys' and, I must say, that is a dreary cold mansion. Lady Tilbury's fires are such inadequate little things, one always freezes. I vow, my hands are near frostbite," declared Sophia, kneeling before the fire and holding out her hands to its warmth.

"I know." Mallory shivered. "I'm so glad I didn't have to go with you today. Was there anyone interesting there?"

"Oh, not very. Jane Tilbury's young captain came in and brought several of his friends, and Beth and Harriet Borely and their mother, dreadful woman."

"Oh, hark at her," said Augusta. "No one of interest, indeed! And how about the handsome duke? Not interesting to you, I suppose?"

Sophia blushed, but refused to rise to the bait.

"What duke was this?" demanded Charles.

"Harold James Allardyce, Duke of Carnmoor! And couldn't take his eyes off Sophia. He greeted his hostess, looked about and saw Soph and made a beeline for her, and so far as I was able to observe, never addressed another word to anyone else the whole time!"

"Oh, Augusta, how can you say so? Why, you talked to him yourself, and he was very interested in all you had to say."

"Not he! I would be surprised if he had been able to repeat one word of the conversation five minutes later. He had a sort of stunned look in his eyes."

"Gussie, dear, you know how you are prone to exaggeration. It's all a hum, Mallory. You mustn't listen to a word she says."

Mallory couldn't resist teasing Sophia. "Why, what is this, Sophia? Have you trapped a duke, and the Season not even begun yet?"

Sophia, much shyer and more gentle than her twin, obligingly blushed again and protested in vain. Augusta told her she was a dissembling, missish thing and began tickling her. Charles pulled Mallory back down into his lap again to watch the romp.

Mallory had every reason for smugness about the conditions of her life. Raised in much luxury, she had been forced at eighteen to seek employment, when her father's death revealed him penniless. Charles had hired her by letter to go to Linbury and take charge of his twin sisters, and during this period Charles had fallen in love and married her. He had immediately brought her mother and younger sister to Linbury to live, relieving her of the terrible responsibility of their support.

Having successfully transformed Sophia and Augusta from unkempt imps to young ladies of fashion, she had steered them through their first Season, and could congratulate herself for their success. And now to have this added bliss of carrying Charles' child! It seemed to her that life could not be more wonderful.

The girls' tickling match had finally come to a breathless end, and the two girls lay on the floor in front of the fire and quiet descended again on the comfortable room.

A log collapsed, rousing them all from their pleasant stupor.

"One of you put another log on," Charles requested the twins drowsily.

But Mallory stirred and announced that they must all go and dress for dinner.

"Can we not have a quiet evening to ourselves?" Charles protested.

"No, my love. You know we are promised for dinner at the Aylesburys'. Girls, bestir yourselves, now. Have you decided what you will wear?"

She finally succeeded in herding them all up the stairs, the girls to their room and Charles into the hands of his valet. Clara, Mallory's own abigail, was waiting for her with hot water and Mallory's pomona-green gauze laid out on the bed.

The twins, resisting Beth's pleading, were ensconced on their beds, pondering the problem of what to wear. Beth had been with them in Linbury, and now, after two years, felt quite proprietary about her two young mistresses, and familiar enough to let her own opinions be known.

"The pink satin, Miss Sophia, 'twill best become 'ee, and the green for Miss Augusta."

"No, Beth, not the green, for I saw Mallory's green

laid out on her bed. I'll wear the white," said Augusta firmly.

The twins had finally succumbed to Mallory's strong feelings about individuality, and now never dressed alike. Orphans since the age of five, they had grown to use their sameness as a weapon, as protection and security. But with Mallory's help, they had gained enough confidence to want to stand apart as two separate people and be valued each on her own merits.

"Soph, do you think your duke will come to the Aylesburys' tonight?"

"Please, Gussie, don't tease. You know he is not 'my' duke. We have but met for a few moments."

"But you liked him well, I could see."

"Oh, yes, I thought him everything that is handsome and gentlemanly."

"Jane Tilbury says the old duchess is a dragon, guards her precious son like the crown jewels."

"Oh, dear, I hope I shan't have to meet her!" exclaimed Sophia.

"Meet her?" giggled Augusta. "If you flutter your eyelashes at him another time you may find you have her for a mother-in-law!"

"Gussie," said Sophia warningly, moving towards her sister with fingers outstretched.

But Augusta laughed and rolled away to the other side of the bed.

With two great fires roaring at either end of the large drawing room, and hundreds of candles, the Aylesburys' guests were in no danger of frostbite as the Tilburys' guests had been during the afternoon. Lord and Lady Aylesbury were both rotund and jolly, and obviously able to order every luxury for their comfort and the pleasure of their guests.

The Portman party found, as they entered the room, a crush of people already assembled, and, from the pitch of conversation rising all around them, having a jolly time.

The Honourable Caroline Waugh came rushing up to embrace the twins.

"My darlings, how famous that you came! I was afraid you might not. Isn't this a wonderful squeeze, and so early in the Season! But then, Lady Aylesbury's parties are always madly successful so that one hates to have missed them. Now, which is Augusta and which Sophia?"

"I'm Augusta. Sophia's wearing the pink tonight, and we're doing our hair differently."

"Very becoming, too. You must get Beth to show my maid how to do it. I'm afraid she's not very creative with coiffures yet."

"Now you're fishing for compliments, Caroline, for well you know you are looking beautiful tonight. My dear, where did you find that delicious shade of rose?" asked Sophia.

"How lovely of you to say, Sophia. Did you know that Carnmoor has been invited?" said Caroline, with a knowing glint in her eye. Sophia turned and pretended to be looking for someone in the crowd. She was determined not to blush or become flustered, and so to have Augusta accuse her of acting missish. But Caroline was not in the least deceived by this, and continued, undeterred.

"You haven't met the old duchess yet, have you? Wait till you see! She has the most quelling eye I've ever encountered. Makes me quite shrivel up every time."

"Is she looking for a wife for him?" asked Augusta bluntly.

"I think if she has her way he'll never marry. No one could possibly be good enough for him. I find him charming of course, and oh, *so* handsome, but I wonder if he is not spoiled beyond hope by such adulation," said Caroline.

"Well, we shall soon know, for if I'm any judge, he's smitten with Sophia."

"Oh, Gussie, please do not say such things. We spoke but a few words this afternoon. How mortifying for one, if he should be cool tonight after you spread such word about—" begged Sophia.

Augusta was instantly contrite. She knew her twin to be much more sensitive than herself, and also that her own teasing sometimes went too far.

"How stupid of me, Soph. Of course, you are right, and I promise you I won't speak of it again. And when he comes, I shall disappear, so that he will be sure to find you. It wouldn't do to get him confused between us."

Sophia laughed softly, "Oh, no fear. He says he has no trouble telling us apart. He says he can tell by the way we speak."

"The way we speak? Why, what can he mean by that? We speak the same."

"He says not," said Sophia, with a secret smile.

"Well, you will have a chance to prove it one way or the other in a moment, for he has just come in with his mother," said Caroline. Sophia started visibly and dropped her eyes, but Augusta turned around and boldly studied the newcomers. The young man was searching the room eagerly, and when his eye fell on Augusta, from his point of view completely hiding Sophia, he smiled. Bending to excuse himself to his mother, he came across the room to them.

When he came up, Augusta held out her hand and he bent to kiss it and then to look into her eyes warmly.

"I am so glad you could come, Miss Sophia," he said fervently.

"Oh, I would not have missed one of Lady Aylesbury's parties. One always has such a lovely time," she responded.

A light frown showed itself on his face and he just looked at her for a moment without answering. Then his face cleared and he smiled again.

"Oh, forgive me, Miss Portman, I mistook you for your sister. Is not Miss Sophia with you tonight?"

At this point Sophia stepped forward to stand beside the completely flabbergasted Augusta, and held out her hand to the duke, with a smile that only verged on the triumphant.

Chapter Two

Mallory, nibbling on a piece of toast and sipping her tea at breakfast the next morning, was sorting through the stack of invitations that had arrived.

"Well, Sophia, here is one that should interest you. Her Grace's compliments, and the Duchess of Carnmoor would be pleased to receive me and my sisters, Miss Portman and Miss Sophia Portman, this afternoon. Shall we go?"

Sophia had already pushed back her chair and come around to inspect the note for herself.

"Oh, good heavens, what shall we do? I don't think I could take her in her own drawing room. When Carnmoor introduced me to her last night, my knees were shaking, so I could hardly drop her a proper curtsey. She stares at one so coldly."

"Pooh," declared Augusta, "she didn't scare me. I just stared back at her, till she finally gave up. You must stand up to people like that, Soph."

"Well," temporized Mallory, "I agree that one mustn't allow people to intimidate one. On the other hand, Augusta, you could get a reputation for pertness if you carry such things too far."

"Oh, I didn't stare at her impertinently. I just opened my eyes very wide and stared at her *innocently*. She might think my wits had gone astray, but she could not really accuse me of being rude."

"Don't be too sure, Augusta. Her Grace is not exactly a want-wit herself. It wouldn't surprise me to find she had you pegged to the inch. However, the question is, will we go?" Mallory looked questioningly at the girls.

"Mallory, will you mind very much? I—I—think we—I know that Carnmoor would like it if we did," faltered Sophia.

"I will not mind at all. It is settled, then? I must be off. I've an appointment with my mantua maker. Would either of you care to accompany me?"

But the girls had engaged themselves to ride with Caroline Waugh and her brother this morning, and flew off to change into riding dress.

When the Portman carriage drew up in front of the residence of the Duchess of Carnmoor that afternoon, three extremely stylishly dressed ladies descended and made their way to the door. Sophia's pelisse was trimmed in ermine and Augusta's in sable. Mallory wore a scarf of sables over her shoulders. The early April weather still carried enough nip in the air to make them grateful for the fur, as a sharp wind tugged at their skirts. Fortunately, they were not kept waiting, for a most impressive butler opened the door at once and bowed profoundly. He led them directly into the drawing room, and announced them.

The old duchess, sitting in a massive chair beside the fire, treated them all to her stony gaze, but condescended to extend her hand to Mallory.

Her son, however, more than made up for his mother's lack of warmth by kissing each of their hands, and smiling sweetly upon them. He then turned to introduce them to other visitors in the room.

"Mrs. Wixton, you will allow me to present Mrs. Charles Portman to you, and Miss Portman and Miss Sophia Portman," he said to an extremely sharp-featured elderly lady, who smiled as though it were costing her something in pain to so move her mouth. She was attended by her son, whom the duke introduced as Mr. Bramforth Wixton. Mr. Wixton, in total contrast to the hatchet-faced emaciation of his mother, was round and pink. His eyes, rather too close-set, blinked at them sleepily for a moment, and then he performed an elaborate bow which involved several flourishes of his lace-trimmed handkerchief. The girls carefully avoided each other's eyes.

Mallory was invited to sit beside the duchess, and she was subjected to a rather blunt interrogation. Where was their estate? Where was their townhouse? Why did Mr. Portman's sisters not dress alike? Since they were twins, duplicate dress would be so much more effective. Mallory politely dealt with her inquisitor, while Mrs. Wixton held Augusta captive and the duke led Sophia to the other side of the room, obstensibly to view a painting.

He pointed out some of its finer qualities, although he found it difficult to take his eyes from the much more entrancing picture presented by Sophia beside him.

"I'm afraid I know little of such things, Your Grace, though it is a very pleasant painting, is it not?" said Sophia shyly.

"Sophia—no, do not look shocked—I intend to call you Sophia from now on, and you will call me Harry, as all my friends do."

"Oh, I don't think—" protested Sophia.

"Nonsense! I don't hold with such formalities. We are friends, are we not?"

She nodded shyly, her eyes cast down. "But I fear your mama will think it very forward of me and will not like it at all."

"Never mind about Mama. I will explain it all to her. She's not a bad old thing at all, you know."

"I find her rather—rather—awesome," admitted Sophia.

"Pooh, Sophia. You must not let yourself be intimidated in this way. I'll wager your sister does not."

"Oh, no. Augusta was always much braver than I. We were used to get into some terrible scrapes as children, and she was always unafraid."

Now Harry had always been just such a brash, impetuous youth himself, and he turned to look at Augusta with more interest than he had heretofore accorded her. From the first, he had been attracted to Sophia's softness and seeming pliability, but he couldn't help hoping that her qualities were not indicative of a lack of spirit. He admired spirited girls, who gave some sparkle to flirtations. Though, so far, none of the ones he had met had quite taken his fancy as Sophia had. Her soft brown eyes and delicate profile had seemed to him more beautiful than those of any girl he had ever seen. When he had then been presented to her sister, he had indeed, as Augusta declared, looked stunned. But it was only at the picture of *two* such faces. However, he had turned from Augusta's cool regard back to the sweet smile of Sophia, with some relief at their first encounter. He had thought Augusta arrogant. Being somewhat arrogant himself, he had no trouble recognizing the quality in others. But now he thought that perhaps he had mistaken Augusta's more aggressive attitude—he thought perhaps her lack of intimidation was a sign of courage, and he admired courage.

Augusta, meanwhile, was suffering agonies of boredom under the sour smile of Mrs. Wixton, whose whole conversation consisted of disparaging remarks about anyone she had come into contact with.

"Oh, you are a friend of Caroline Waugh? Well, she is a taking little thing, I admit, if you like that style. However, for me she is just a bit *farouche*. Do you agree? Not enough polish, but then, her family—who were they, after all? Jumped-up cits, if you ask me."

"Oh, surely you are mistaken, Mrs. Wixton. The Waughs were a prominent family when the Conqueror came first to London."

Mrs. Wixton sniffed at this, and passed on to see what damage she could do to the reputations of various other of her acquaintance. The only person not touched by her acid tongue was the Duchess of Carnmoor.

"My dear, Her Grace and I have been friends since we were girls together, always in each other's pockets forever. I'm sure the dear duchess will tell you herself that she confides everything in me. Such condescension."

Augusta could not help feeling sorry for Her Grace, if such were the case, for she could not think of anything more unpleasant than having Mrs. Wixton forever at one's side. She looked around with a sort of quiet desperation to see if someone would rescue her.

Carnmoor had just turned to look at her and caught the rather wild look in her eye. He stifled a laugh, and taking Sophia's arm, led her back across the room.

"Come, we must rescue your sister, who has not done anything so bad as to merit the punishment of another moment of Mrs. Wixton's conversation."

"Ah, Your Grace, I was just telling Miss Portman how close your dear mama and I have always been," cried Mrs. Wixton as they approached, baring her yellow teeth in her most flirtatious smile.

"Yes, just so," he rejoined noncommittally. "Miss Portman, your sister and I hold differing views on my new painting. We would like you to arbitrate the point for us." And he dexterously extracted Augusta from her tête-à-tête and led both girls back to the painting.

Augusta, her back safely turned to the horrible Mrs. Wixton, began to laugh helplessly and silently. "Oh, that horrible woman. Your mother must find her a great trial. I know I would," she spluttered when they were out of earshot.

"You may take my word for it my mother knows perfectly how to squash all Mrs. Wixton's pretentions. They have known each other since they were children, and my mother feels sorry for her for some reason. Mrs. Wixton drove Mr. Wixton to an early grave, and he most thoughtlessly left them less well off than they had hoped. I should warn you both that she is on the lookout for an heiress for her son, so it would be best to pretend to be poor little country mice. Of course, if you have any warm feelings towards Bramforth—"

Augusta shuddered delicately. "He didn't speak at all,

but he does rather devour one with those little piggy eyes. One thinks at first that he is dozing off standing up, but every time one looks at him he is sure to be leering."

Harry laughed, "Yes, he does rather fool you with that sleepy air, but he takes in everything going on, I believe. At balls he is always to be found dancing with the prettiest girls, but when it is time to go down to supper he makes sure his partner is some antidote with a dowry of at least thirty thousand pounds. I have heard him declare that anything less would be a waste of his time."

"Oh, dear," said Sophia. "I do hope he will never ask me to dance. I never know how to refuse people like that."

"I simply stare them in the eye and tell them I am already promised, even if I prove it to be a lie by sitting quite alone throughout the dance," said Augusta, laughing.

"I must be sure to keep your strategy in mind, Miss Portman, if you should refuse me one day," said Harry.

"I'm sure that if Your Grace were so condescending as to ask me, I would be too overcome with the honor to think of refusing," she replied solemnly.

"I am sure you are never overcome by anything, Miss Portman," he riposted with a straight face.

"Well, not often, but one lives in expectation," she answered.

Sophia, looking from one to the other during this exchange, hoped they were not disliking each other. Her own open nature made it impossible for her to judge the undercurrents she felt passing between them. There was a certain edge to it that made her hurry to step in and smooth things over.

"Gussie, you must call him Harry, and he shall call you Augusta. He does not like too much formality and says I must call him so, and if I do, why, so must you," she smiled.

Harry bowed and Augusta nodded, and the matter was settled. Before they could continue the discussion, they were summoned by the duchess to attend her.

When their guests had all departed, the duchess looked

thoughtfully at her son, standing at the fire, seemingly entranced by the flames.

"Well, Harry, have you a *tendre* for one of those gels?" she asked bluntly.

"I think them charming, but you must know I have only the briefest acquaintance so far."

"Who is this Charles Portman, their brother? I don't believe I have ever been acquainted with any Portmans."

"I believe the parents died when the twins were but five or so. The father was Edmund, I think, and their mother was a Stowerton."

"Letitia Stowerton! I should have realized—she looked very like the girls. Yes, now I do remember something of that tragedy. But they are very wealthy, are they not?"

"Very, so I have heard. Their dowries are in the neighborhood of fifty thousand pounds."

"Good heavens, don't let Amabel Wixton hear of that. She'll set that stupid Bramforth on them."

"So I have warned them. But I think they can handle Bram. At least Augusta can, and she will take care of Sophia."

"Yes, Augusta. Now there's a gel I could bear to become better acquainted with. Nothing missish about her, no simpering and blushing. Looks you right in the eye. I like that."

"Dear Mama, you are rather forbidding, you know. It isn't that Sophia has no spirit, she just—"

"Lacks gumption. However, I make no quarrel with Miss Sophia. She's a pretty-behaved child. I also found Mrs. Portman much to my taste, and discover that I was well acquainted with her mother many years ago. Flavia Tolgarth. Lovely woman with real spirit."

"Well, I am happy my friends meet with your approval. Most gratifying. I'm afraid I can't say the same for all of yours. How you can put up with that dreadful Wixton woman is beyond me. Not to speak of the despicable Bram."

"Now don't come down too hard on Amabel. If it weren't for me, I doubt the poor soul would get invited anywhere, and they are dreadfully bad off, you know."

"Well, if she craves company, she should learn to curb her tongue. I've yet to hear her say a nice thing about anyone. I would wager you anything you like that she is at this moment tearing the Portman ladies to pieces."

But in this Harry was wrong. Far from tearing their reputations apart, she was ruminating quietly to herself as the duchess' carriage, kindly put at her disposal, carried her homeward, her son slumbering beside her.

She had heard rumors of the sizable dowries of the Portman twins and had been very eager to meet them today. She saw that Harry seemed to have his eye on Sophia, and she speculated that it would be no bad thing for Bramforth to cultivate Augusta. That girl was less pliable than her sister, and that of course was to be regretted, for Mrs. Wixton had no mind to have a headstrong daughter-in-law. However, there were compensations. The girl was undoubtedly a catch, if the rumors were true, and she was certainly presentable enough. But best of all would be the alliance with the Duke of Carnmoor. Why, Bramforth and Harry would be brothers-in-law! With this thought she sat up straight and poked her sharp elbow into the soft, padded ribs of her son.

"Wh-a-a? What is it? I wish you will not dig your elbow into me in that way, Mama. I have asked you many times. You will do me an injury one day."

"Wake up, Bramforth. I have something important to say to you."

"Could you not have waited until we reached home? I would have had to wake up then in any case," he grumbled. But he sat up and adjusted his hat and pulled down his waistcoat.

"The thing is, I've been thinking. You could do worse than pay attention to Miss Portman. She is a lovely young woman, and, I've heard, extremely well dowered."

"Hm-m. Yes, she's a pretty piece, right enough," he agreed, his small eyes beginning to gleam with interest. "How much?"

"I don't know yet, but you may rest assured I will make it my business to find out in the next few days. I

22

think you should pay a morning visit to the Portmans' soon."

"I think that can be managed," he agreed graciously. "I'm hungry. Do we dine out tonight?"

"No."

"Drat," he said, with a gloom based on too-long acquaintance with the inadequacies of his mother's underpaid cook.

Chapter Three

The past three days of halcyon weather had sent all the Portman women scurrying about to refurbish their wardrobes with dimities and lawns, and the carriages parading in the Park billowed and fluttered with pastels and ruffles.

Mallory hurried downstairs one morning after a footman had come to tell her that a Lord Armstead was calling. She rushed into the drawing room, her hands outstretched.

"Dear Courtley, how very nice to welcome you to London. Have you been in town long?" She greeted him with her warm smile.

"Just came in late yesterday, and made this my first stop, naturally. Where are the girls?"

"I sent word for them to come down as soon as they finished dressing. Do sit down, my dear, and tell me all the news. How is your dear mama?"

"Flourishing. I tried to get her to come in with me for a visit, but now that she has your mother there at Linbury,

I don't know whether she can be budged. Those two are forever in each other's pockets."

"How wonderful for my mother to have found her old friend."

"Courtley!" exclaimed Sophia, rushing into the room, her eyes alight with gladness.

He rose and went to take her hands, stared into her eyes for a long moment and then bent to kiss each hand fervently.

"Sophia!"

"Oh, Courtley, how wonderful that you have come. There are ever so many things planned, we shall have such a fine season."

Augusta came in to add her welcome, and they all sat down to gossip about their country neighbors.

Courtley could hardly take his eyes from Sophia, who looked truly fetching this morning in a gown of primrose lawn, which set off her brown eyes to perfection. Augusta, in blue-sprigged dimity, looked equally pretty, but not to Courtley.

The butler announced Mr. Bramforth Wixton, and he came into the drawing room to be greeted by three pairs of dismayed female eyes and Courtley's curious gaze. However, so great was Bramforth's self-esteem that he did not notice a lack of warmth in his reception. He had dressed very specially for this occasion and assumed what he saw was amazement at his splendid appearance. It *was* amazement that gradually overcame their dismay, for his coat, in a startling shade of blue, sported unusually large round buttons, and his fat face and several chins were supported by shirt points and cravat that seemed to make it impossible for him to lower his head or turn it. He performed his elaborate bow.

"How kind in you to receive me, dear Mrs. Portman. I could not withhold from myself the pleasure of calling to see Miss Portman."

Sophia and Augusta exchanged a look. Sophia was happy indeed that the accident of birth had caused it to be Augusta who was first-born, and therefore heir to the title of Miss Portman. However, to her alarm she discovered Mr. Wixton bearing down on *her*.

He arrived in front of Sophia, possessed himself of her unwilling hand and planted a kiss upon it.

"Your servant, Miss Portman. I have thought of you continuously since our fortituous meeting at the dear duchess' several days ago."

Sophia pulled her hand away in confusion, casting a pleading glance at Augusta and then at Mallory.

Mallory took charge. "Mr. Wixton, you are addressing Miss Sophia Portman."

Undismayed, he turned, without a word of apology, to Augusta and went through the same performance, word for word.

Augusta, her lips twitching, heard him through, and then introduced Courtley to him and asked him to be seated. He lowered himself gingerly onto the edge of a sofa, his fear obvious on his face as to the reliability of his already endangered pantaloons. Everyone carefully looked away and all burst into conversation at once.

"Lord Armstead, do you make a long visit in London?" interrupted Bramforth pompously.

"For some weeks, I believe. And you?"

"Oh, I am forever here. My mother and I do not find the country agreeable. We try to go to Bath when the social life becomes too much for us here. Just for a rest from it all, you know."

"I see," said Courtley politely, and turned away to speak to Sophia, leaving Augusta to deal with this ridiculous man.

"Mr. Wixton, are you not enjoying our fine weather?" said Augusta, bravely facing the inevitable.

"Lovely indeed, Miss Portman. I had thought if you had some errands, I would offer myself as your escort. A stroll through the streets might not come amiss on such a fine day, to take advantage of the weather."

"You are all kindness, Mr. Wixton, but it will not be necessary to trouble you."

"No trouble at all, I do assure you, my dear Miss Portman, no trouble at all." He waved away such a small thing disdainfully. "I know you young ladies are ever in a quest for ribbons and fripperies."

Augusta, feeling that this conversational avenue had been fully explored, made no answer and for a moment could think of nothing to say.

"How is your mother, Mr. Wixton?" interposed Mallory, coming to Augusta's rescue.

"Tolerable, Mrs. Portman, tolerable. She was waiting for the Duchess of Carnmoor, who had very kindly offered to take her for a drive in her carriage this morning," he informed them grandly.

"How lovely for Mrs. Wixton," responded Mallory. "Is it not, Augusta?"

"Yes, lovely," she said somewhat lamely. *Really,* she was thinking, *What does this pompous man want with me? Surely, he cannot think that I gave him enough encouragement at the duchess' to have occasioned this visit. We hardly spoke a word together. In fact I don't remember that he spoke at all.*

Bramforth was thinking that his mother was as smart as she could stare. This was as fetching an article as he'd seen in London in many years, and if they could get the true information regarding how much money came with her, her wouldn't mind making her an offer.

These edifying thoughts were interrupted by yet another visitor. The butler announced that His Grace, the Duke of Carnmoor, wondered if they were receiving. He was bid to show the duke in at once.

Harry strolled in smiling, and stopped short to find that others were here before him. He stared interestedly at Sophia and Courtley, sitting side by side on the sofa, looking very intimate indeed, and then his eyebrows rose at the sight of Bramforth Wixton.

Harry came forward to bend over Mallory in greeting and then turned to Augusta, before turning to Sophia.

"Harry, good morning. You will allow me to make you acquainted with Lord Armstead, our neighbor from the country," fluttered Sophia.

Courtley stood up and the two gentlemen bowed to each other politely.

28

"Sophia," said Harry, "I have come to request the pleasure of taking you for a drive this afternoon."

Sophia became even more flustered. "Oh—well I—the fact is, you see, I've already accepted Lord Armstead's invitation to drive this afternoon."

Harry smiled politely and turned to extend his invitation to Augusta and Mallory.

"Thank you, sir, but I am engaged to Lady Tilden this afternoon," responded Mallory.

Augusta, seeing Bramforth about to speak, and fearing he would extend an invitation to her, rushed to accept Harry's invitation.

"Wonderful, Harry. Just what I would like of all things. The Park must be delicious today, and I'm sure everyone will be out," she said enthusiastically.

"Why, Miss Portman, I was just on the point of asking you. I'm sure Harry will understand. Will you not, Harry?" Bramforth protested.

"Decidedly not!" said Harry promptly. "You were just too slow off the mark, Bram."

"Well, really, Harry. I call that very high-handed in you. Ah well, not to worry, perhaps we may still come about. What say you we make it a threesome? You could just drop by and take me up on your way to the Park."

"Sorry, Bram, I'm taking the phaeton, you see. Room for two only," said Harry blandly.

The talk continued in a more general way after this. Bramforth contributed little to the conversation, but sat stolidly, staring at Augusta most of the time in what he was convinced was a most compelling way. He was so convinced of this that he did not notice that she almost pointedly ignored him.

It soon became apparent to everyone that he was determined to outstay the other gentlemen, however long that took. Harry, with a rueful smile at Mallory, finally gave him best and took his leave, promising Augusta he would call for her at two o'clock.

Shortly after this, Courtley also said his goodbyes, with a like promise to call for Sophia immediately after luncheon.

Still Bramforth sat, unmoving, blinking sleepily at Augusta. Actually, he was hopeful of being invited to stay for some nuncheon, if he waited patiently enough. Mallory, Augusta and Sophia bravely attempted to engage him in conversation, but the going was very heavy. Bramforth disliked being required to contribute in a social situation, for the simple reason that he could rarely think of anything he could be bothered to say.

Mallory finally realized what his strategy must be, and, determined not to be so put upon, even if she had to be rude, rose.

"Mr. Wixton, you must excuse us. Our dressmaker is waiting upstairs, and her services are so in demand now that one dare not keep her waiting."

Bramforth recognized defeat, and, rose rather grumpily, and with no apology, to his feet.

When the door closed behind him, the three ladies looked at each other in silence until they heard the outer door close, and then all burst into hysterical giggles.

"Oh, *what* an odious man!" said Augusta, sitting up finally and wiping her eyes.

"Mallory, you are so wonderful. I vow I could not think of a single thing to say to him. People like that paralyze me," said Sophia.

"Well, I could see he wanted to be invited to take his luncheon with us, but I could not bear the thought of sitting through a meal with him. Really, I cannot find a trace of sensitivity in him. I don't think I've ever met such a totally self-centered man in all my life."

"Was it not shocking in him to have asked Harry to take him up in his carriage?" asked Sophia.

"And how relieved I was to hear Harry say no. By the way, Sophia, I hope you don't mind that I accepted? I could see that Mr. Wixton was opening his mouth to speak, and was so terrified he would invite me out for a drive, I jumped at Harry's invitation."

"Of course I do not mind. But I don't think you need have worried. I don't believe the Wixtons keep a carriage. At least, I am always hearing how the duchess takes Mrs. Wixton everywhere, or sends her home in her carriage."

"You are probably right. Which makes it worse. He would probably have invited me to go for a *stroll* in the park!"

Mallory had departed for Lady Tilden's, and Courtley had driven away with Sophia, when Harry finally helped Augusta up into the seat of his high-perch phaeton.

"How dashing!" cried Augusta enthusiastically. "I've longed to ride in one of these."

"You are not afraid?"

"Afraid? Pooh, what should I be afraid of?"

"Well, some ladies find the height disconcerting and refuse to be driven in one."

"Oh, I like it of all things! I wish I could drive one myself."

"I would be happy to teach you."

"*Would* you?" breathed Augusta, her eyes wide. "You are not just teasing me?"

"I would not tease about something so serious. I will be around tomorrow to give you your first lesson. We'd best make it first thing in the morning, when there won't be so many spectators about."

This settled, they turned to other subjects, their talk often interrupted by the many acquaintances they met. The roadway was filled with a line of carriages going in either direction, and many young gentlemen on horseback. Presently, they passed Courtley and Sophia, moving along sedately in Courtley's open landau. Harry flourished his whip at them and the rest all waved gaily to each other. Sophia looked radiant, and Augusta wondered if Harry would notice how happily she seemed to be going along without him.

"This Armstead, he's an old acquaintance?" he asked Augusta.

"Oh, we've known Courtley this age. We practically grew up together. He was our only friend at Linbury for a long while, when we were barefoot and straggle-haired devils. That was before Mallory took us in hand."

"Hmmm. He seems much smitten with Sophia. Does she return his regard?"

"I'm afraid you will have to apply to Sophia for the answer to that," she replied coolly.

"I beg your pardon. That was an ill-mannered question, I agree. Let us speak of something else. You have made a conquest, I noticed this morning," he teased gently.

Augusta gave him a startled look, and then when she saw the glint in his eye, she began to laugh.

"I may have. We can't be absolutely sure. You see, he has not yet figured out which of us is which. But, of course, we are both overcome with the honor."

"Only natural," he agreed solemnly, "if he gets it all sorted out, you will allow me to be the first to congratulate you, will you not?"

"I will probably be unable to restrain myself and will rush into the streets with the good news," she laughed.

Bramforth reported to his mother that he had followed her advice and paid a morning call upon Miss Portman.

"Did she seem receptive to you?" his mother asked.

"Oh, indubitably. All warmth and graciousness. I don't think there will be any problems," he said confidently.

His mother looked at him with approval. "I knew she would take to you, Bramforth. You are all charm when you will extend yourself."

"Did you find out how much she's worth?"

"Not less than fifty thousand, I'm told by a most reliable source."

"Very nice. Very nice, indeed. Then I think I will pursue it. I'm rather hampered by not having a carriage, you know."

"We can't run to a carriage, Bramforth. You will just have to make do without. Perhaps I could give a little dinner for her."

Bram shuddered. "No, please not that. Your cook would not be up to it."

"Well, then, what say you to a small supper at Vauxhall Gardens? We can do very well there for not too much money, and there is the dancing and the fireworks, so one is not put to the trouble of entertaining."

"Yes, that might be the very thing. Do you arrange it

with Mrs. Portman. We shall not have to invite both girls. Just Miss Portman and Mrs. Portman, don't you think?"

"Oh, I agree. It would be a waste of money to take Miss Sophia along. I will call upon Mrs. Portman tomorrow and arrange it."

Chapter Four

The smart, high-perch phaeton swept without checking around the sharp curve in the road and the landau approaching the curve from the opposite direction, whose horrified driver had frantically hauled on the reins to bring his carriage to a complete stop.

Augusta flicked her whip back, and with a very showy twist of her wrist caught the tip with the same hand and turned to give her passenger a triumphant smile.

Harry, apparently completely relaxed, had never betrayed by so much as a flicker of an eyelid, the heart-stopping peril of the maneuver she had just completed. He thought now of the wild-eyed terror of the other driver and of Augusta's obliviousness of it, and he could not help smiling back at her. Her cheeks were rosy and her brown eyes flashing, and she looked altogether beautiful.

"Well, sir, and was not that well done?" she asked with a happy laugh of excitement.

"Oh, you are a regular out-and-outer, Augusta. I doubt I could have done it myself."

"Truly, Harry? How kind of you to say. And so kind to give me so much of your time this way. I daresay it is really boring for you to have to just sit by and watch."

"No, no—not—*boring*," he said with twitching lips.

"And such a good teacher, never criticizing or being nervous," she continued.

"But you are a most apt pupil, Augusta, even though you take your corners a little tight still. However, I make no doubt you will master it with more practice."

"Too kind. What do you mean I take my corners too tight? I did not take that last corner too tightly at all. Perhaps you did not notice?"

"Not notice!" He looked at her in amazement, then threw back his head in a roar of laughter. "Well, I may have been diverted for just a moment by the look on the fellow's face who was turning from the other direction. But only for an instant, I assure you."

"Why, what can you mean? What look on his face? We were miles apart and he had plenty of room. In fact, I did just wonder why he had stopped at all. Cowardice, no doubt, or inexperience."

"You are absolutely right, my dear. After all, it was but the merest flake of paint scraped off, and he cannot be so small-minded as to complain."

"No such thing," she exclaimed indignantly. "I came nowhere near him. Stupid fellow, to sit there gawping in that way."

"I had put it down to sheer terror, but no doubt you are right, and it was only stupidity."

She flashed him a look of protest, only to find him smiling broadly at her. The corners of her mouth curled up in spite of herself and finally she could not help beginning to giggle.

"Just the same, it was great fun to make a corner like that without checking. Oh, I do wish I could persuade Charlie to buy a carriage like this."

"Perhaps when he sees how well you drive he can be persuaded. My mother was an expert whip also in her day, you know, and she had to learn in secret. However, when my father saw her drive, he said she did him proud and bought her a new carriage and a pair of the finest matched grays I've ever seen."

"I should like to have seen her then. She is a wonderful lady, even though she pretends to be forbidding. I think it's just her game, and she's secretly laughing at us as we shake in our boots in her presence."

"You have it exactly, Augusta, that is exactly what she does. And the people she most admires are the ones who are on to her game and stand up to her."

Augusta nodded in satisfaction. "There, I knew as much. I like that. I shall be just such an old lady myself, I'm sure."

He studied her flushed face for a moment. "Yes, I think you will be. You are very like her actually. Very like her as she used to be, I mean. Beautiful and spirited."

Augusta turned to look at him, too startled by the compliment to think of anything to say. For a long moment they stared into each other's eyes, then in spite of herself, Augusta felt the warmth of a blush spreading up from her neck, and looked away in confusion, busying herself with her whip and the reins.

"Will you be attending the Coleshires' dinner party tonight?" she finally contrived to ask, hoping she had achieved the light tone she was striving for.

"No, fortunately. They have a most uninspired cook, and the daughter is always 'persuaded' to sing; her mother is doing that girl a disservice by forcing her in that way, for she has no talent. Will you be attending?"

She laughed, "Actually, we were going as a family, but now I think I will be too overcome with the headache to attend."

"Very wise. I should pull up your leader just a shade if I were you," he advised.

She quickly followed his instructions and they bowled along quietly for a few moments. Harry was content just to be with her and to watch her face. He was trying to puzzle out how it was possible for two people to have such an exact resemblance as Sophia and Augusta and yet be so entirely different in personality. Sophia was all gentleness and sweetness, while Augusta was witty and high-spirited. Could it be that the first twin was selected by nature to lead the way from the safety of the womb to the unknown dangers of the waiting world, because of inborn intrepidity, while the second was fated always to be the more timid, the follower? Not necessarily without courage, but lacking forcefulness, he mused, thinking of Sophia, and trying to imagine her sitting here with him, learning to drive a high-perch phaeton. No, it was a picture he could not conjure up. As Sophia had said herself, she took no pleasure from danger, while he could easily imagine Augusta leading the way into every sort of adventure.

Augusta, hearing a carriage approaching from behind, cast a glance over her shoulder.

"Ah, another perch-phaeton! I wonder if he would be interested in a race?"

"Augusta! You will do no such thing. This is but your third lesson, and while I admit you are doing admirably, I cannot allow a race just yet."

"Oh, how disappointing of you, and I was convinced that I was quite the expert," she said, her face falling.

"You are indeed, but young ladies racing perch-phaetons might not be looked upon with favor by the rest of London society. And I'm sure Charlie would not approve at all. If you are to impress him, you must show him that you are prudent as well as expert."

"Yes, I suppose I must," she replied, but still unable to keep her disappointment from showing.

Harry laughed delightedly, "Augusta, you are entirely fearless, and wholly adorable. I'm sure you've heard that before."

"Well, a few times," she answered demurely.

"And still on the shelf? I wonder at the enterprise of the younger generation. I should have thought you would have been snapped up your first Season."

"Well, I have had my share of offers, but so far none to my taste, I fear. I seem always to attract the placid types, like Bramforth Wixton. Sophia has always more appeal to the sort of man I—" she stopped abruptly, appalled at what her rash tongue had been ready to reveal. She became very concerned suddenly with the business of giving way so that the gentleman behind her could pass, and hoped fervently that the import of her last sentence had escaped Harry.

Sophia, in pink-sprigged muslin and parasol to match, sighed contentedly as she rode along in Courtley's open landau. The warm sunshine and the green of the grass and the wealth of flowers glimpsed here and there gave her a feeling of being back in the country.

"Oh, Courtley, do you not miss home? I would love to be back there now," she exclaimed.

"Very much, but then you would not be there, even if *I* were, so I don't wish it," he answered, carefully not looking at her and trying to sound casual.

"Of course. I must be here for the Season, I suppose. But I must confess that I prefer the country and our own provincial entertainments to the grand balls and the formal dinners here. I am truly a country mouse, I fear."

"I find it agrees with me better also. More comfortable in every way."

"Oh, much!" she agreed fervently. "If I were home and saw grass so green and smooth, I would simply take off my shoes and walk in it, as I long to do now!"

"The very thing! A nice barefoot ramble to the secret pond, and maybe a swim."

She giggled, "Oh, Courtley, it is not warm enough yet to swim. But it would be nice. Well, the season will soon be over, and we will all be back and can do those things." She said this last with such a wistfulness in her voice that Courtley turned to look at her, somewhat startled. He knew, of course, of her preference for the country, but he had thought her in the midst of being courted by Harry, and, he would have thought, not eager to be parted from him. But then, perhaps, they would not be parted, for undoubtedly Harry would come for long stays at Linbury. This thought caused Courtley to resolve to find a great many visits to pay to friends in other parts of the country this summer. He could not bear to hang about and watch Sophia being courted by, and by that time probably engaged to, Harry Allardyce, no matter how fine a fellow he was.

"Courtley," said Sophia hesitantly, "have you developed a *tendre* for Jane Dilworth?"

"Jane Dilworth?" he asked with astonishment, "well of course not, how can you think so?"

"Only that it seemed to me that I am forever seeing you with her—riding and dancing and—well, I wondered."

"But I ride and dance with many other young ladies, including yourself," he added, attempting gaiety.

"You do not mind that I asked? It is only that I think of you as my best friend, and am always so comfortable with you that I feel I can say anything."

"Best friend," he said flatly and somewhat absently.

"Why yes, Courtley, we have always been so, have we not?"

"Yes, of course, my dear," he said hastily, unable to deny her anything, even love for another man, if it made her happy.

"Oh, Courtley, do stop. Just see that delightful little grove there. Let us get down and explore it. There are daffodils, and I feel sure there must be violets under those trees," she said eagerly.

Courtley obliging pulled up and they clambered down. Courtley found a violet and picked it to present to her with a flourish.

"Thank you, sir. My first violet of the season. Do you remember when we would pick them and plait them together to make crowns? I always felt like a queen with such a crown."

"And looked like one, Sophia," he responded warmly.

"Did I, Courtley? How kind of you to say so. You never told me that before."

"Well, at the time, I was much too doltish to say things like that."

"More probably you did not think such things then,"

she laughed, "I doubt boys do, ever. Girls do, of course; we're romantics from birth, I believe."

"Well, that may be so, but it seems to me I remember two hoydenish girls who disdained fairy tales and genteel behavior as missish. They even put hair-brushing under the heading of silliness and time-wasting."

She laughed delightedly. "We were terrible, weren't we? We used to skulk about in the woods and pretend we were knights defending a castle, and dream of how wonderful it would be to be boys. We wanted to run away to sea at one point, I remember, and spent days trying to figure out how to get boy's clothes to disguise ourselves in."

"Well, those were really romantical notions, whether you thought so or not. But I'm glad you changed your minds and decided to be girls."

"Oh, I think Mallory must take the credit for that. I've often wondered what would have become of us if she hadn't come into our lives. At first we resented her terribly, and felt we could win out against her, but she was up to all our tricks," Sophia laughed, "and now see how happily everything has turned out."

"Has it, Sophia? Are you happy?"

"Well, of course I am, Courtley. Don't I seem happy?" She looked at him in genuine puzzlement.

He took her hand and pressed it. "I only wanted to make sure. I want you to be happy always."

"Dear Courtley, you are so kind to me," she smiled up at him.

He stood looking down at her dimpled face, wishing that he had not sworn to himself that he would not speak to her of his love until she had had a chance to get through two Seasons and meet a reasonable number of other men. He had been wise enough to realize that the unformed young girl he had fallen in love with would probably have responded to him if he had declared himself at the very beginning. But she then might regret not having had the life other young girls of her station in life were entitled to: Seasons in London, balls and parties and the opportunity to meet many young men. He had wanted her to turn to him with as much certainty as he felt, when finally the moment came. Now he wondered if he had lost his chance entirely. She seemed to have fallen in love with Harry, and he was helpless to do anything about it.

He longed to cup that sweet face in his hands and kiss her soft mouth and tell her all he was feeling. But he was afraid it would turn her friendship for him to disgust—if she were indeed in love with Harry.

No, I must bide my time, he decided resolutely, if mistakenly, and held his arm out for her to lead her back to the carriage.

Chapter Five

"O moon, thy pale and limpid beams
Are far outshone compared to gleams
Of those two silvery stars in my mistress' face"

Mrs. Charles Portman suppressed another shuddering
yawn, and widened her eyes in hopes that the tears it
caused would not be too apparent. She forced herself to
look interested and appreciative at the foolishness being
intoned to her by Lord Beaumont, kneeling at her feet,
parchment in hand, reciting his latest paean of praise to
her beauty. She was aware that she was really most un-
grateful, and wondered yet again if it were some deficiency
in herself—perhaps a lack of sensitivity—that caused her
to be so overcome with boredom when she was forced to
listen to these outpourings.

She was aware that she was the envy of her wide circle
of acquaintances for being the inspiration—the muse—
of such a handsome young poet as Lord Beaumont, but

she couldn't help feeling they would not envy her so much if they were made to listen to it.

He commenced the third stanza and she allowed her mind to drift away, wondering if she could find the sort of batiste she had in mind to make a robe for the baby, and just what kind of embroidery she would put around the tiny neck. A particularly impassioned line caught her wandering attention, and she turned to smile benignly upon him in encouragement. He was but nineteen, after all, and far too beautiful to be a boy. Actually, it would have been kinder if Fate had given those eyelashes to his sister, a rather pale, insipid girl, she thought. From the vantage of Mallory's twenty-two years and impending motherhood, she couldn't help looking down upon him as a foolish child. However, it was the fashionable thing to have a young man pretending to be hopelessly in love with one, and a harmless pastime, after all. But she did find it unfair that one had to be bored to death to be fashionable.

Lord Beaumont paused in mid-sentence as the drawing room door opened to admit Williams, the butler. Mallory looked up eagerly, praying there was another caller to save her from what she felt sure, from the size of the paper Lord Beaumont was holding, could only be another eight stanzas. When Williams announced Mrs. Wixton, Mallory found herself rising to greet her with a warmth that was entirely the product of the ennui of the past-half-hour.

"My dear Mrs. Wixton, how very nice to see you. Do you know Lord Beaumont?"

That young gentleman looked completely astounded that anyone could be so mannerless as to interrupt his deathless poetry. But years of training by his mother forced him to rise and bow to the lady with good grace.

"Lord Beaumont, how do you do?" said Mrs. Wixton, her smile revealing teeth that a more discriminating person might have preferred to keep covered.

"Very well, madam, I thank you," he replied, averting his eyes from this unappetizing display and shuddering delicately.

Mallory was well aware that his every sensibility had been offended, but so weary was she of his company she could only be grateful to Mrs. Wixton for coming to her rescue.

"I do hope I have not interrupted you, Mrs. Portman," cooed Mrs. Wixton, "but as I was passing, I felt I must just stop and have a small visit."

"Only too happy, Mrs. Wixton," said Mallory, in what she hoped was not too fervent a tone. She glanced nervously at Lord Beaumont, but he was reading his ode to himself with such rapture that he had forgotten them entirely.

The ladies seated themselves and began to chat of mutual friends, Mrs. Wixton inserting "the dear duchess" into every other sentence, then gradually adding the name of her darling Bramforth to sentences in between.

"And where is the beautiful Miss Augusta this morning?" inquired Mrs. Wixton finally, feeling that it was time to edge the conversation around to the real purpose of her visit.

"Why she is being given a lesson in driving by Carnmoor, I believe."

"The duke! Why—why—how unusual. Do you think it wise, my dear, to allow such a thing?"

"Such a thing as what?" Mallory inquired coldly.

"Well, I mean, he drives a perch-phaeton, does he not? Surely no well-brought-up young lady would be seen driving such a carriage."

"I cannot think why you should say so, Mrs. Wixton. I distinctly remember seeing Lady Sarah de Gray driving just such a carriage in the park last Wednesday."

"Just the same, my dear Mrs. Portman—and besides, you know what *her* reputation is? I have heard that she—"

"Mrs. Wixton," Mallory interrupted firmly, "will you take some refreshments?"

"No, no, Mrs. Portman, though I thank you. You will forgive me for it if I seem to be inferring that your discipline may be somewhat lax with the twins, dear Mrs.

Portman. After all, I am so much older that I think I may be allowed to know better."

"Not at all, Mrs. Wixton. However, it is not necessary. I have not found Sophia and Augusta in need of any disciplining from me. They have never given me any cause whatsoever. Far from disapproving of Augusta's learning to drive a high-perch phaeton, I am delighted. In fact I so envy her that I might try it myself."

"Well—of course, Bramforth would never approve."

"I'm afraid I don't understand you, Mrs. Wixton. What could he possibly have to say to the matter?"

"Oh, well, you see, dear Bramforth has developed such an interest in your dear Augusta that—"

"Very flattering, I'm sure," Mallory beyond caring if she was rude, changed the subject. "How do you find the Duchess of Carnmoor these days? Is she in health?"

"Exceedingly well, Mrs. Portman, thank you," replied the unsnubbable Mrs. Wixton, with a proprietary air. They proceeded to a discussion of topics of a less inflammable nature, exchanging notes of social affairs they had attended, and recent news of engagements and weddings. Finally Mrs. Wixton broached the object of her visit.

"Have you been to the Vauxhall Gardens, Mrs. Portman?"

"Well, not this season, though last fall we made up a party to go there."

"I had thought it would be most delightful if you and Miss Portman would be my guests one evening for a small supper there."

"Well—I—well, I'm sure that is very kind of you, Mrs. Wixton, but I don't—"

"Ah, you are thinking that I should ask dear Mr. Portman and Miss Sophia to accompany us? But I'm sure you will understand how it is, Mrs. Portman. My circumstances, you see, do not permit me to entertain so large a party, and yet, I cannot deny myself the happiness of entertaining altogether. So I must limit my guests to suit my means, don't you see."

Now of course, such a speech was well calculated to make Mallory seem churlish if she refused, indicating that

46

she was insensitive to Mrs. Wixton's lack of funds, and mean-spirited to deny her pleasure. Mallory could only murmur understandingly, "Of course, of course," while casting about wildly for some excuse to refuse.

"I had thought Friday evening, if that would suit," pursued Mrs. Wixton.

"Oh, I *am* so sorry," Mallory babbled gratefully, "but we are all engaged on Friday to the Diltons."

"Saturday, then."

"Saturday is the Wembleys' ball, Mrs. Wixton, and we are promised—"

"What is your first free day, Mrs. Portman? We are perfectly amenable to whatever day is agreeable to you," said Mrs. Wixton, inexorably.

"Well, I shall have to consult with Augusta, of course—" Mallory was defeated, and she knew it. She could only hope that previous engagements would make it impossible for them to settle upon a date, until this tiresome woman forgot the entire scheme.

At this moment, the drawing room door burst open to admit Augusta, cheeks aflame with color and eyes sparkling.

"Oh, Mallory, you must really try it! I like it of all things. One is so high, and there is really nothing to it, I vow." She came to an abrupt halt at the sight of Mrs. Wixton peering around the chair with her teeth-baring smile.

"Augusta, my dear, here is Mrs. Wixton come to call, and Lord Beaumont," she added hastily, searching around the room, having totally forgotten that he was still there. He rose from the windowseat and bowed gracefully, then sat back down and continued reading. Augusta, completely deflated, came forward to greet Mrs. Wixton, albeit reluctantly.

"Miss Portman, I have just been telling your sister how much I hope to entertain you with an evening at Vauxhall Gardens. We are but settling the date now, so you came at a most fortuitous time. What evening will you be free?"

Augusta cast a wild-eyed glance at Mallory, and received one of apology in return.

Mrs. Wixton plowed determinedly on, "Will Monday night suit both of you?"

"Monday night?" faltered Mallory, looking at Augusta. "Well, if you are free, Augusta—"

Augusta resigned herself. "Whatever you say, Mallory."

So it was settled, and the hapless Portman women were engaged to sup with the Wixtons, whether they would or not. Mrs. Wixton triumphantly took her leave.

Mallory and Augusta looked at each other helplessly, and Augusta smiled ruefully.

"On the whole, I think maybe I prefer the son to his mother," she confessed in a low voice, so that Lord Beaumont wouldn't hear. But Beaumont moved into the middle of the room, raised his eyeglass, and stared at the door closing behind Mrs. Wixton, as though her image were imprinted upon its panels. Finally he dropped the glass and turned to Mallory with a look of wide-eyed astonishment.

"Who *is* that dreadful person?" he asked in awed tones.

"You know perfectly well, Beaumont," replied Mallory crossly. "I introduced her to you when she came in. She is Bramforth Wixton's mother, and I know you have met him."

He held up his hand, "Please, say no more. I try never to let ugly thoughts intrude. It disturbs the flow, don't you see."

Augusta giggled, and Mallory relaxed and smiled at him. She had only been cross because she felt so guilty in having allowed Mrs. Wixton to force them into complying with her wishes. Mallory felt that she had betrayed Augusta by not handling the situation better.

"Augusta, I am so sorry to have let you in for this."

"Darling, I'm sure you had no choice, and besides you are let in for it also. Perhaps we shall contrive to have a good time in spite of them. There are bound to be other people one knows there."

"You are most forgiving. No doubt you are in such high spirits because you have been doing something daring."

"Oh Mallory, you've no idea how exhilarating it is.

You really must try it. I wonder if we could persuade Charlie to buy us a high-perch phaeton?"

"I would think it highly unlikely, my dear. I don't suppose Sophia would like it at all," she said thoughtfully.

"Not at all, I should think," replied Augusta.

"Perhaps you should suggest it, just the same," said Mallory thoughtfully.

"But I don't think she—oh—yes, I suppose you may be right." Subtly the glow receded from her face, and as Mallory watched it go, she felt a twinge of worry. Was it possible that Augusta had developed a *tendre* for Harry? If so, what could possibly be the outcome but a great deal of unhappiness for the poor child, since Harry himself had, so far, shown a marked preference for Sophia? And what of Sophia? From all that Mallory had observed, it seemed obvious to her that though Sophia might not be aware of it herself as yet, she looked happiest when she was with Courtley.

Oh dear, thought Mallory, *now what should I do? Shall I say anything more? Perhaps it won't be necessary after all,* she decided, taking another cautious peek at Augusta's face. Augusta was exceedingly clever at picking up the unspoken thought, and from the looks of her now, she had picked up Mallory's inference regarding Sophia and Harry.

Augusta, staring into the fire, was sternly suppressing the pictures of various moments shared with Harry during the driving lesson. *Mallory is right,* she thought, *Harry is only being kind to me because of Sophia, and I must not allow myself to get into the way of thinking of him in any other way than as a beau of Sophia's.*

At this point, Lord Beaumont, having made several momentous deletions and changes in his manuscript, rose and sauntered over to join them at the fire.

"Dear Mrs. Portman, I think all is now perfection. May I continue? I feel sure the last five stanzas will far surpass the first five in your estimation."

"What? Oh, Beaumont, I beg your pardon. Do you not think it would be best to leave it for now and—"

She was saved from having to think of a further excuse

by the entrance of Charles who strode straight across the room to Mallory, apparently unaware of the presence of anyone else. He picked her up in his arms and swung her around.

"And how is my darling wife? Have you missed me all morning? What have we for luncheon? I'm starving," he said, all in a rush as he swung around. He suddenly became aware of Lord Beaumont standing there, his mouth slightly agape, and of Augusta, seated by the fire.

"What is this? You still here, Beaumont? I saw you coming in as I left. Never tell me you're still reading your bit of verse?"

Lord Beaumont clutched his manuscript protectively to his chest with both hands, with such a look of pain mixed with outrage at hearing his masterpiece referred to in this fashion, that Augusta had to put her hand over her mouth to conceal her smile, while Mallory contrived to hide her face against Charles' coat.

Sophia and Courtley walked into this scene, and stopped in amazement at the sight of Charles holding Mallory in his arms and facing Beaumont, as though some very dramatic scene were being played out.

Lord Beaumont looked at these new arrivals, and apparently decided against so large an audience. He bowed with a sad smile, and strolled from the room with great dignity.

Chapter Six

Monday inevitably arrived, and with it an effusive note from Mrs. Wixton. Mallory, reading it at breakfast, took a sip of tea and nearly choked when she began to laugh. Charles came around the table and pounded her on the back till she begged him to stop.

"Oh, that odious woman! She is truly capable of anything," Mallory spluttered.

"I just know you mean Mrs. Wixton," said Augusta darkly.

"Just so. She is so eagerly looking forward to this evening, she says, and it occured to her that since we must be taking our carriage anyway, would it be an inconvenience to pick them up on the way? Such fun to all arrive together, she says, and in any case, I must know that her circumstances make it impossible for her to keep a carriage."

"Mallory, are you sure you don't want to beg off this ridiculous expedition?" asked Charles. "I could always come down with a mysterious fever and need you at my bedside."

"Thank you, my love, but if we don't go tonight, she will somehow get us another night. Best get it over with, don't you think, Augusta?"

"Unfortunately, yes. However, I suppose we can comfort ourselves with the thought that we don't have to do it again."

"Oh, Gussie, how depressing for you to spend an entire evening with those people. I'm sure I would dislike it intensely. Not even seeing the fireworks could make up for it," declared Sophia.

"It might not be too bad, Gussie," offered Charles. "Bram rarely utters, and if you could just think of some way to keep Mrs. Wixton from smiling too much—"

"Now you think to tease me, Charlie, and I warn you I won't stand for it. All very well for you to feel smug, you'll be safe home."

"Yes, Charlie, don't tease. I'm sure Gussie is too brave for words," shuddered Sophia. "I wish there were something I could do to help, Gussie."

Augusta looked at her thoughtfully for a moment. "Well, Soph, there is something you could do."

"Only tell me, darling, you know I will help if I can."

"You could go in my place and pretend to be me."

Sophia looked at her in horror. "Oh, Gussie, do not ask it of me."

Augusta laughed. "Don't be such a wet goose. As though I would. Now never mind, both of you. Mallory and I are prepared to take our medicine, and we shall have a grand time in spite of the Wixtons, will we not, Mallory?"

When the ladies stepped out of their carriage after Mrs. Wixton, on the land side of the Gardens, they were still very much of a mind to have a gay time. The party made its way through the paths towards the Pavilion, where they were to hear the concert. The Gardens were like an enchanted land, with thousands of fairy lights strung everywhere, and entwining walks leading in every direction.

Bramforth found seats for them, and they listened to

the orchestra through the first half of the concert, and then decided to forgo the delights of the Rotunda, since they had all witnessed the spectacles there the previous season. Mrs. Wixton had reserved a supper box for them, and they settled into it to await what turned out to be a delicious meal. Meantime, there were throngs of people passing to and fro, affording Mrs. Wixton plenty of opportunity to exercise her sharp tongue. She kept up a steady stream of chatter into poor Mallory's ear, while Bramforth, after doggedly eating his way through a large meal, exerted himself ponderously to be agreeable to Augusta.

"Grand place, this, do you not think so, Miss Portman?"

"Yes, it is truly delightful, Mr. Wixton."

Bramforth contemplated her reply for a moment, then replied, "Yes."

He rested for a few moments after this effort. Then, at a sharp nudge from his mama, which elicited an irritable glance from him, he spoke again.

"You are looking very elegant tonight, Miss Portman," he offered, his piggy eyes leering at her.

"Too kind, Mr. Wixton," replied Augusta uncomfortably.

"Perhaps you'd care for a stroll?"

"*No!*" she exclaimed, then realizing she had responded a bit too vehemently for graciousness, "Thank you, but not now, Mr. Wixton, if you don't mind."

"Not at all, Miss Portman, not at all." He relapsed back into silence for a while, and Augusta turned with pretended animation to Mallory and Mrs. Wixton.

"Isn't it lovely, tonight, Mallory? So many people, too. I do believe I just saw the Tildens. Perhaps we will see them again later. Such fun, Mrs. Wixton."

"So glad, dear child. Now I know you young people will want to be off exploring, so do not hesitate to leave us. We will do very well here. Bram, perhaps Miss Portman would like to see the Fountain of Neptune."

Augusta cast Mallory an anguished glance, but knew she could expect no help from that quarter. Willing as Mallory might be, she was clearly no match for the very determined Mrs. Wixton. Bramforth was now standing behind her chair, and with a great feeling of martyrdom, Augusta arose. Bramforth held his arm with elephantine gallantry and there was nothing left for her to do but take it.

There were other, and certainly more suitable looking couples, also strolling about the paths, and in some of the darker arches could be heard low murmurs and gay tinkling of laughter. Augusta devoutly prayed that she would encounter no one she knew.

Mr. Wixton paused beside one of these darkened niches, and seeing it unoccupied, led her inside and asked her if she would not care to sit for a moment. Augusta prepared for the worst. She was not afraid that she could not defend herself against any advances from Mr. Wixton, but the very thought was so offensive. However, feeling that this was obviously the point of the whole evening forced upon them by Mrs. Wixton, she decided that on the whole it might be better to get it over once for all.

Bramforth sat down beside her and possessed himself of one of her hands.

"Miss Portman, I'm sure you cannot be unaware of my growing feelings for you."

Augusta drew her hand away. "Mr. Wixton, you will oblige me by not saying anything more."

"Ah, I see how it is. Very nice, too. I approve of such maidenly modesty."

"I assure you it is not modesty, Mr. Wixton, but I would not have you waste your time any further."

"My dear, I could never feel that I have wasted any moment spent with you," he returned, with a heavy flirtatiousness.

Augusta rose, "I think we had best return to the others now, if you don't mind, Mr. Wixton."

Bramforth rose and seized her hand again in his. "Do not speak now, Miss Portman. Just give me hope that I—"

"Mr. Wixton, please!" said Augusta, tugging vainly to release her hand from his clutch.

"I have been too hasty, I can see that now. All young girls like to be courted. Well, courted you shall be, Miss

Portman. You will forgive my precipitousness this evening. Charge it to my eagerness, to the growing feeling I have for you that will not be denied."

"Mr. Wixton, I don't know where you can have developed this great feeling, since we have met but twice."

"Ah, Miss Portman, I knew the moment I first saw you, and persuaded myself that you were not unwilling to receive my attentions."

"Then you persuaded yourself wrong!" snapped Augusta, patience at an end. She rapped his knuckles sharply with her fan, causing him to release her hand, and turned and hurried away down the path back to the supper box, Bramforth panting along in her wake.

When they arrived at the box, Mallory knew with one glance what had happened. Augusta had a high, angry color in her cheeks and her eyes flashed sparks. She flounced angrily into her seat and deliberately turned her back on Bramforth. Mallory saw Mrs. Wixton raise her eyebrow interrogatively at her son, and he sketched a slight shrug. Mallory held her fan to her mouth to hide her twitching lips and began to talk to Augusta of all she had seen while they were away. Gradually Augusta calmed down, and finally turned to give Mallory a speaking glance, to which Mallory returned a deliberate wink. Augusta relented at last and smiled back.

"Mallory," came a voice, and they all turned to see an extremely handsome young man advancing upon them, hands outstretched.

"Good heavens, Alesdair!" responded Mallory, holding out her own hand. He bent to kiss it, and then stood smiling warmly at her. Mallory, slightly flustered, pulled her hand away and turned to meet the avid gaze of Mrs. Wixton.

"Mrs. Wixton, you will allow me to present to you Lord Hastings, a very old friend. And this is my sister-in-law, Lord Hastings, Miss Portman, and this gentleman is Mr. Bramforth Wixton. Mr. Wixton and his mother are entertaining us this evening to supper."

Lord Hastings kissed the ladies' hands and bowed to Bramforth, then turned back to Mallory.

"You are married then, Mallory? Who is the fortunate man?"

"My husband is Charles Portman. And what of you, Alesdair, are you not married in all this time?"

"Not I. It was a near thing more than once, but I've escaped unscathed so far," he declared with a most engaging twinkle in his dark blue eyes.

"Why, the last I heard—was there not a Miss Coverly?"

"Alas, she found another whose pockets were not quite so much to let as my own."

"You were always a wicked rogue, sir, and have not changed one bit."

"Nor I have. You must know, good people, that this beautiful lady took possession of my heart years ago, and I have never been fit for female companionship since." He turned to Augusta. "Would you care for a stroll to see the fountain of Neptune, my dear Miss Portman?"

"Why, thank you, Lord Hastings, but I just returned from—er—seeing it. However, is it not time for the fireworks? Perhaps we could all walk along and find positions to watch them."

This was agreed upon, albeit somewhat reluctantly by Mrs. Wixton, who had not had it in mind to have her party taken over by a handsome man.

However, Lord Hastings held an arm for Mallory and Augusta and led them away, leaving nothing for the Wixtons to do but follow tamely along behind.

Augusta, completely recovered from the unpleasantness with Bramforth, was tremendously amused by this gay and dashing man. He flirted with both of them equally and outrageously, and never for one moment said anything that anyone could take the least exception to, in contrast to the crude fumblings of Bramforth.

They were all suitably impressed by the fireworks, and clapped delightedly as the fountains of light sprayed against the midnight blue of the sky.

Meantime, Mrs. Wixton, under cover of the noise about them poured a tirade of abuse into the ear of her son. What had he done? Had he made any move? None? Stupid boy, what did he think she had sent them for a stroll for?

He had what? Idiot! Much too soon for that. Had he no finesse at all. She had thought him experienced in these matters. Had she to coach him in everything? And on and on and on. Poor Bramforth, much chastened, could only stand and try to defend himself.

The evening finally came to an end. Lord Hastings bid them all good night, promising Mallory he would call tomorrow to renew their acquaintance, and to meet her husband.

The Wixtons were dropped at their door, and Mallory and Augusta, with deep sighs, fell back against the comfortable squabs of the carriage and began to discuss the evening.

They found Charles and Sophia waiting up for them, and had to recount the events of the evening to them. When Augusta told them of her expedition with Mr. Wixton, the rest began to laugh, and the more she said the more they laughed. Finally, she began to find it funny, and joined them. So the evening, as they had prophesied in the morning, turned out to be an extremely gay one for Mallory and Augusta.

After they had all retired for the night, Charles came to his wife's room, dismissed her maid, and took her into his lap.

"Now, tell me about this Hastings fellow," he demanded.

"Oh, Charles, you idiot. I've told you about the Hastings fellow. Now tell me about you. Did you miss me?"

Charles told her in the best possible way of how he had missed her.

Sophia and Augusta, in their own room, were also talking of Lord Hastings, with Augusta describing his looks enthusiastically.

"Augusta, never tell me you're interested in him?" asked Sophia eagerly.

"Never! Oh, I admit he is a charming fellow and fun to be with, so witty and entertaining, but too frivolous for my taste. I can see why Mallory did not accept him."

"Such fun to meet an old beau of Mallory's. Do you think he will call tomorrow?"

"Sure to. It's my belief he is still in love with her. You can see it the way he looks at her, like a starving man at a full table."

"Oh, no, Augusta. What will she do? What about Charlie?"

"Ha. Nothing to fear there. Those two don't know anyone else exists. Besides, Lord Hastings can't hold a candle to Charlie."

"That's true. Darling Charlie." And much comforted with this thought, Sophia curled down to sleep.

Chapter Seven

Sophia was engaged to ride with Harry this morning, and as she dressed carefully in her new bright blue riding dress with the frog closings, she mused over her feelings for him. They had met almost daily since the first encounter. Either he took her riding, or came for morning calls, and inevitably they met at the various parties and balls that took place in the evenings, now that the Season was in full swing. She invariably danced the first dance with him, and more often than not at least one, if not two, more during the evening. She was aware that in the eyes of most people he was considered to be dangling after her, making her the chief object of his attentions, and an announcement was expected to be forthcoming at any moment.

Naturally Sophia was flattered by these attentions from a man considered the catch of the Season: titled, handsome, young and extremely wealthy. Apart from all of this was his personal charm. He was always gentle and warm with her, letting her see that he considered her the most attractive of women. But there was no denying she was not entirely comfortable with him. He intimidated her in some way, making her feel always inadequate in his presence, as though she were not behaving in just the way he would have her.

Adjusting the blue velvet hat, with the ravishing plume curled against her cheek, she watched Augusta, being buttoned into a lilac morning gown by Beth.

"Gussie, do you find Harry rather—well, sometimes— a bit overwhelming?"

"Overwhelming? What do you mean, dear?"

"Well, it seems to me that he sometimes, for instance when he teases me—is disappointed with me."

"Oh, I expect he wants you to tease him back."

"Well, and so I would, but I'm not always sure until later that he is doing so, and then I can never think of what to say. I'm not as quick off the mark as you are, Gussie."

"Darling, don't fret yourself about it. You are so sweet-natured that no one expects you to be witty also."

"I'm not so sure. I think Harry would prefer wit."

Augusta, being of the same opinion, could think of no reply to this, so she set herself to be soothing.

"Just relax more, Soph, and you will find it more comfortable as you go along."

"But that's just it, you see," said Sophia. "I always find myself blushing and becoming tongue-tied with Harry, even though he is so kind to me always. He is so sort of—dominating—that I begin to feel stupid. I'm never comfortable with him as I am with—" her voice trailed off and she stared into the mirror at her own face, though it is doubtful if she actually saw it.

"Courtley?" asked Augusta, finishing the sentence for her.

"Hmmm," agreed Sophia absently.

As she cantered along beside Harry in the bright April sunshine, she resolved to be relaxed and comfortable, as Gussie had advised. She peeked around at Harry beside her. He was undoubtedly a most prepossessing man, with his lean, dark-eyed good looks and his tall, commanding presence. He was the object of a great deal of attention from other riders, especially amongst the women, who smiled and waved and simpered at him continuously.

"Sophia, would you like to learn to drive my perch-phaeton also, as Augusta is doing?" he asked her suddenly.

"Oh—why, I—well, actually—"

"Actually, no, I take it?"

"I don't think I would even want to ride in it with you."

"I hope it is not the driver who affects you so?"

"The driver?" she puzzled.

"I meant myself, Sophia."

"You? I don't understand you, Harry."

"I understood you to say that you would not want to ride in my perch-phaeton with me, and I said I hoped it was not myself who affected you so," he explained, with only the barest hint of impatience.

"Oh!" She laughed gaily. "Of course not, Harry, how can you say so? I was speaking of the carriage itself. It is too high. I would be very nervous."

"But would you not also enjoy the excitement of doing something that made you just a bit fearful?"

"Why no, why should I do that? There are so many wonderful things to do that don't make me fearful at all."

"I see," he replied, with a slight smile, and dropped the subject.

She knew that again she had disappointed him in some way, and was unable to understand just how it had happened. She couldn't help looking forward to the end of the ride. This afternoon Courtley was to take her to Madame Tussaud's Wax Museum, and she was looking forward to it very much. Courtley was so easy to be with, and she realized now that she had not seen him at all yesterday and had missed him very much.

"Sophia, you and I must have a serious talk one day soon," Harry said now, taking her by surprise again, so that she stuttered.

"T-t-talk? Why, what? Well, of course, H-h-harry."

And now she was more nervous than ever. Was it

possible that he was about to make a declaration? She must prevent it, she thought in a panic, she must let him know in some way that she could never—did not want—what? Did not want him to be in love with her? Did not want to marry him? But was this really true? Or was this just nervousness caused by an impending situation? She had known him just a few short weeks, after all. Perhaps this breathless, panicked feeling was one felt by all young girls on the verge of their first proposals.

But then she thought she was just being silly. After all, it was entirely possible that he had no such proposal in mind at all. She must forget she had even thought of it or she would become sillier than ever in his presence.

She looked up to see, prancing toward them, Courtley with—Jane Dilworth! *Well, of all things,* Sophia thought unreasonably.

"Ah, good morning, Sophia! Carnmoor! Beautiful day, is it not?" called Courtley gaily.

Jane, all dimples and giggles, allowed her horse to curvette about and made a great play of bringing him under control again.

"Well, Armstead, that's a fine piece of horseflesh you have there, a regular goer. Did you bring him up from the country?"

"Yes, my favorite mount, take him with me always if I can."

"Your Grace," interjected Jane to Harry, "will we see you at the Carpenter-Bains ball tonight?"

"Oh, of course, Miss Dilworth, and I will count on your saving me a dance," he countered.

"Happily, sir," she said with a gay laugh.

Now how did she do that? thought Sophia, in bewilderment. *If I had wanted a gentleman to ask that of me I would never have been able to think of a way to manage it. I wonder how many she has Courtley booked for already, since she does it so easily.*

Thinking to take a page from Jane's book, Sophia turned to Courtley.

"And you, Courtley, will you be there?"

"Well, of course, Sophia. Don't you remember we discussed this a few days ago?"

"Oh, so we did," she said, but she was thinking furiously. Why could not have Courtley responded in the same way as Harry had to Jane? Was it in the way it was said, or was it that Courtley didn't know how the game was played any more than Sophia herself did? Not, of course, that she was in any doubt that she would dance with Courtley at the Carpenter-Bains' tonight, but she would like to have proved to herself that she could elicit the same responses as Jane Dilworth if she chose. She decided that this was something she would have to discuss with Augusta, who seemed to have the same ability as Jane.

Mallory, that morning, had felt, for a few moments, distinctly unwell, causing her abigail to run and fetch Charles. By the time he reached her room, the nauseous attack was all over, and she was able to tell him that she had never felt better in her life. And indeed, she had never looked better, with the soft rose color in her cheeks, and her alabaster complexion suffused with a soft glow as though lit from within. Charles sent the maid out of the room, so overcome with love for his wife that he felt he must kiss her. As a consequence of this dalliance, Mallory had still not come downstairs when Lord Hastings made his appearance, carrying two posies for the Portman women. When the butler came to Mallory with news of Hastings' arrival, she sent him to see if Miss Augusta could go down and entertain him until Mallory could dress.

Thus it was that Augusta, rushing into the room, was treated to the sight of a young man's face falling in disappointment at her appearance. So obvious about it was he, that she could only stand and laugh at him.

"Now, sir, I protest you are most unkind." She rallied him. "Is this the way to greet a lady? Are you so rag-mannered that you cannot dissemble just a bit to keep from insulting me?"

He laughed also, "Forgive me, Miss Portman, but it has been so long since I had seen Mallory, and I was very eager to renew old times with her."

"Renew?"

"Reminisce?" he countered.

She nodded in acceptance of this amendment. "Mallory sent me to tell you that she is a bit late this morning and will be down presently. Will you not be seated?"

He extended the posies to her, "Allow me, Miss Portman, one for you and one for the beautiful Mrs. Portman."

"How lovely! Thank you very much, sir."

"I am in hopes that you will both carry my favors to the Christopher-Bains' ball tonight."

"Both of us?" she asked in amazement.

"Oh, yes, and I shall have the pleasure of knowing the two most beautiful women in the room have done me honor," he replied gallantly.

"Very commendable ambition, Lord Hastings. Tell me, you have not met my sister yet, have you?"

"Your sister? Why, no. Do not tell me there is yet another beautiful Portman woman?"

"Oh, indeed, the most beautiful of all," she laughed.

Mallory came in at this point, and Lord Hastings crossed to take her out-held hand and kiss it lingeringly.

"My dear Mallory, good morning. I hope you will forgive my rushing around so early. Put it down to my eagerness to see you again as soon as possible."

Mallory laughed at him gently. "Alesdair, you had always the prettiest speeches of anyone. Now, do you be seated and we will talk."

They all sat down and began eagerly to discuss all the people they had known several years ago when Mallory had made her own coming-out. Since many of these people were still very much a part of the London social scene, Augusta was able to enter into the discussion with no trouble.

Charlie, coming to the door and looking in upon this cozy gathering, felt a stab of jealousy to see his wife, her eyes sparkling with animation, talking and laughing so happily with her old beau. This was a totally unnecessary reaction on Charles' part, since he had momentarily forgotten that but a short time before she had looked just this way with him, and that her glow now was more likely attributable to their lovemaking than to a few moments in the company of a beau she had rejected even before she had met Charles.

She looked up at this moment and saw him, and the smile she gave him was so dazzling that Lord Hastings started and whipped around, to see who could have elicited such a look from her.

"Charles, darling, here is my old friend Lord Hastings come to call."

Lord Hastings stood and held out his hand to take the one Charles was extending to him.

"Well met, sir," said Alesdair with a smile. "I thought I would dislike you on sight, but I find Mallory's taste, as always, faultless."

Charles heard this speech with a look of amazement, and then shouted with laughter!

"Well, Lord Hastings, I see that one must get up very early in the morning to get ahead of you," and Charles clapped him on the shoulder. "Come, sir, I am just going to have a—er—late breakfast . . ." here he cast a swift glance at Mallory, who dropped her eyes demurely—"and you must join me."

Lord Hastings looked horrified. "Do you tell me I've been so unmannerly as to come before breakfast!"

Mallory reassured him. "No, no, Alesdair. Only Charles is so tardy, the rest of us have been up and about for hours. Do let us go and have a cup of coffee with Charles and talk."

They all trooped into the dining room.

While Charles ate a very large breakfast, the talk flew back and forth across the table, of past routs and balls, and of who had been left on the shelf and who had made most admirable marriages.

"Mallory, why don't we have a small party? I think we must owe everyone in town by now," asked Augusta.

"Yes, of course we will," said Mallory enthusiastically. "I have been most negligent, I realize. So many things to see to when one first arrives. When shall we say? Next week? Will that be all right with you Charles?"

"Of course, my love, whenever you say," he replied

agreeably, "as long as you wear that silvery gown of yours with the pink roses. I want to see you in that again."

Mallory laughed with pleasure to think that he had remembered one of her gowns well enough to want to see her in it again. Men generally had an exasperating way of being unaware of what one was wearing, even though women were convinced men only noticed them if their gowns were just so. The "silvery thing" was actually a white spider gauze embroidered with brilliants; it opened over a silvery gray satin. There were dusky rose velvet ribbon streamers from the bosom to the floor, but the only roses were the ones she had worn in her hair. *Yes*, she thought, *I will wear it again, just for Charles.*

Augusta was eagerly discussing just who would be invited to this "small" rout, and could they please have dancing, dear Mallory, if there were enough couples to stand up?

Into this interesting discussion, Sophia made her appearance. Lord Hastings looked up to see her in the doorway, and a look of complete bewilderment crossed his face. He looked at Augusta and then back to Sophia, and then wide-eyed at Mallory, as though only she could explain this to him. Everyone at the table watched him with amusement and then began to laugh.

"I told you you must meet my sister," said Augusta with a giggle.

"Sophia," said Mallory finally taking charge of the situation, "here is my old friend, Lord Hastings, whom I spoke to you of back at Linbury."

Alesdair rose and bowed to Sophia, who, still laughing, held out her hand to him.

"Sir, forgive us for laughing at you. It was really not nice of Augusta not to have explained beforehand how it is with us. We were used to play such tricks, were we not Mallory? But we've given that up now, or at least *I* have," said Sophia, just a bit self-righteously.

"You are a complete hand, Soph. I suppose you explained to Harry before you introduced him to me?" expostulated Augusta indignantly.

"But you know there was no time—" began Sophia defensively, but Charles interrupted.

"The truth of the matter is that though you neither of you go out of your way to hoax people anymore, you don't mind watching their faces when they happen unaware on the situation. Now that's enough of that. Sophia, we are planning a party, so sit down and help us."

"A party! Oh, wonderful. When shall it be, and who shall come? Will we have dancing?" asked Sophia, taking a chair, and eagerly they all began to make suggestions at once. A small, select group, they decided, that would make it unnecessary to invite the Wixtons.

Chapter Eight

Mallory's first party of the season had grown from a small select group to a gathering of over seventy people. The twins had such a large circle of acquaintances by now, and her own and Charles' was just as large, and somehow there was always another person who would be insulted if not invited. Others made it impossible for Mallory not to invite them, by hinting so openly that they knew of the plans and were wondering that they had not received a card as yet, that Mallory had no recourse but to extend the invitation with good grace.

One invitation had been extended with less than good grace. Mrs. Wixton, always the first to know of everything that happened in town, came hurrying around for a morning visit as soon as word came to her ears. She made no bones about her purpose, telling Mallory that Bram was so looking forward to it, though she herself had been previously promised to the duchess for an evening of whist with some old friends. Mallory could only accept the inevitable, even though with a lack of cordiality, and be grateful that she would only have to receive one Wixton.

Now, as she stood at the top of the steps greeting her guests, she saw that Bramforth had presumed upon her hospitality by bringing a guest of his own. She had never seen the spotty youth at his side, but decided on sight that she did not care for him. His eyes were too pale a blue, and too knowing, his mouth too loose-lipped, and formed into a sneering smile, and his manner when Bramforth introduced him, too oily. All of this would have been enough to prejudice her, but hearing his name put the cap on it.

"Mrs. Portman, you will not mind my taking the liberty of bringing my dear friend with me. He has just come up to town but today. Mr. Bruce Coverly. I believe you are acquainted with his sister, Lady Balfount. She was Letitia Coverly."

Mallory extended her hand, but her nod was cold. She did indeed remember his sister. Letitia Coverly had been engaged to Charles when they first met, and a more artificial, unpleasant creature she had never encountered. Fortunately, Charles had soon become aware of his mistake, and at the same time Letitia had met Lord Balfount, and the engagement had been broken. It seemed difficult to believe that this unprepossessing youth could be the brother of the exquisitely beautiful Letitia, but not at all difficult to accept that such a person would be Bramforth's best friend.

Lord Hastings, advancing up the stairs, caught the slight moue of distaste on her face as she watched them walk away, and laughed.

"Ah, you've met the despicable Bruce, I see. I remember just such a feeling in myself when first I made his acquaintance, as I now see reflected on your face."

"Alesdair! How nice to see you. Yes, he is rather revolting, is he not? That he is Letitia's brother is even more difficult to conceive."

"Yes, she certainly captured all the good looks in that family. And he is just as unpleasant as he looks, I can tell you. During my—acquaintance—with the beauteous

Letitia, I came to know him rather well. In fact, I suppose I am in his debt to some extent. It was he who informed his sister that she was wasting her time with me. When he came to me for a loan and I could not accommodate him, he learned the true state of my finances. She dropped me immediately and turned her attentions to Lord Balfount, poor devil."

"I can only be grateful that she didn't capture *you*, Alesdair, for I'm sure she would have made you miserable."

"No doubt, as I'm sure she's doing to poor Balfount at this moment. His estates cover a large portion of the north of England, I've been told, and he spends most of his time there. She must be foaming at the mouth with rage at being forced to spend most of the year there with him, instead of queening it over London society as she had hoped to do."

When Mallory was able finally to join her guests in the ballroom, she found the dancing already begun, and Sophia and Harry leading the first set, with Augusta standing up with Courtley. Both girls were in blue tonight, though of different shades and design. Sophia's dress was a pale blue gauze, and Augusta's a celestial blue silk. They both looked enchanting with their fair curls and sparkling brown eyes.

Charles, seeing Mallory enter the ballroom with Alesdair at her side, now came to join them.

"Mallory, my dear, I distinctly remember a discussion about this party being a small affair. There must be nearly a hundred people here. I believe it might almost be classified a squeeze. I'm afraid I will never be able to dance with all the ladies I should honor this evening," Charles complained good-naturedly.

"Yes, well, it did rather get out of hand, I'm afraid. Some people had guests staying, who, of course, one had to include. And some," she said with a dark look in Bramforth's direction, "just brought a guest anyway. Did you know Letitia's brother, Bruce Coverly?"

"No, though I knew of him, and what I knew was not very nice, I'm afraid. He had gotten into trouble with a

71

kitchenmaid at his mother's country house, before he was fifteen."

"And several even more unsavory episodes since your time," said Alesdair. "At any rate, he is one of your uninvited guests tonight."

"The devil he is! Who brought him?" exclaimed Charles, his brows drawing together in a frown of displeasure.

"Bramforth Wixton, of course. One could almost know that Bramforth would be friends with a type like that," said Mallory.

"Hastings, you and I shall have to keep our eyes on that young whelp tonight," said Charles grimly.

"Oh dear, what a very unpleasant task, to be sure," laughed Alesdair, "but I will do my best."

Augusta, aware that Bramforth was staring at her with his beady eyes, refused to look in his direction at all, hoping to stave off the meeting as long as possible. She wondered who the frail, unattractive sprig with him could be.

She found out soon enough, for though she made a point of walking off the floor on the opposite side of the room from Bram, he wasted no time in circling around to join her. He took her hand in his possessively and kissed it moistly, then introduced her to his very good friend.

Bruce also bent to kiss her hand, and before Bram could say another word, requested the honor of standing up with her for the next dance. Bramforth looked indignant for a moment, but then decided it was too much trouble to make an issue of it, and subsided. Augusta was reluctantly led to the floor. She loathed him immediately, and found it more and more difficult to be polite. Each time they came together in the dance, she was forced to accept his slightly cold and damp hand, and his smirking compliments, always presented with a leering innuendo.

When the dance ended, she nodded coldly and walked away, without waiting to take his proffered arm, and came face to face with Sophia. Since Bruce smiled and came forward, obviously expecting to be presented, Augusta had no recourse but to introduce them. He immediately requested the honor of a dance, and Sophia acquiesced with her usual sweetness.

Bramforth now claimed his dance with Augusta, and she gave in with as much grace as possible.

"Miss Portman, you are enchanting tonight. I'm sure I shall have my work cut out to get my fair share of your attention," he said as he led her onto the floor.

"It is not at all necessary for you to be put to any work at all, Mr. Wixton," she replied indifferently.

He squeezed her hand conspiratorially, "Ah, but we both know how important it is for me to make such an endeavor, Miss Portman."

"We do?"

" 'Pon my soul, Miss Portman, you cannot any longer be in any doubt of my intentions," he said, puffing slightly from the exertions of the dance.

"Nor can you be in any doubt about mine, sir. I believe I made myself quite clear at our last meeting."

"Ah, I see how it is, you think to trifle with me, but I am a very serious man, Miss Portman, and I would have you know it."

"And I would have you know that I do not like this conversation, Mr. Wixton. You will oblige me by dropping the subject at once, or I shall ask you to excuse me for the rest of the dance."

Bramforth looked about to see if anyone had overheard this forthright speech. No one was looking directly at them, but he felt uneasily that it must have been heard and decided that the girl must be playing some devilish deep game and that he had best say no more for the present. He would consult Mama before taking the next step, or perhaps Bruce could give him a tip on how to go on. Bruce had had a great deal of experience with women.

In fact, though Bramforth did not stop to think of it, Bruce's experience with women had all, so far, been with serving girls. He was but eighteen, and had been a constant source of anxiety to his mother, not to mention her expense in finding suitable husbands for the serving girls in her employ whom Bruce had honored with his attentions.

However, Bruce thought of himself as a fine fellow, irresistible to the ladies, and had come to London prepared to bowl over the fair sex with his charms. These charms he was now attempting to practice on Sophia, with indifferent success.

Sophia, though repulsed by his looks and manner, was too afraid of hurting his feelings to give him the sharp set-down he deserved for the suggestive remark he was making to her. She tried instead to smile politely and pretend not to understand what he was saying.

"You are uncommonly pretty, Miss Sophia. I vow you fairly make my blood boil just to look at you."

"Too kind, Mr. Coverly," said Sophia, looking about the room.

"I make no doubt that I'm the envy of half the young gentlemen in the room tonight, with such a delicious armful as you."

"Oh, you are being nonsensical, Mr. Coverly. Would you mind if I asked you not to hold my hand quite so tightly, sir? It is becoming quite painful."

"Oh, I say, how thoughtless of me. But I cannot help myself, you adorable minx. Here." He lifted her hand to his mouth. "I will kiss it and make it well."

She pulled her hand away. "You will forgive me, Mr. Coverly. I find it too warm for dancing. I will ask you to take me to my sister," said Sophia, feeling that she was being rude, but unable to endure another moment of his company.

"But of course, my dear Miss Sophia. Come, I will find you a quiet place to sit and recover yourself."

And so saying he lead her off the floor, and with unerring instinct led her, before she was quite aware of what he was doing, into a small alcove at one side of the room, set about with several small sofas. The drapes of this alcove had been pulled back so that it was not in any way shut off from the ballroom, but nevertheless it was not a place where a well-brought-up young lady would go alone with a gentleman. He led her to a sofa to the

74

side of the doorway, one that was not in full view of the ballroom and pressed her down firmly.

"Shall I fetch you a glass of lemonade?" he asked, bending over her solicitously.

"No, thank you very much," she replied faintly, looking about in dismay, and wondering how she had gotten into this situation.

He seated himself beside her and took her hand. She pulled it away and began to rise. He stood up instantly and put his arm about her waist and pulled her roughly to him. She raised both hands against his chest to push him away, but he was much stronger than she, and only laughed at her futile efforts.

"Yes, yes, you lovely thing, a little spirit makes it all the better. You want to be overcome, I'll wager. And I'm just the fellow who can oblige you there, for there's nothing I like so well as overcoming—"

At this point Sophia rapped him sharply in the face with her fan, whispering fiercely at him to stop it at once. She was hopeful that she could yet escape without attracting the attention of any of the guests.

He gave a high-pitched whinnying giggle, now so overcome with excitement by her struggling that he forgot entirely where he was.

"Delicious creature, I should like to gobble you up completely. Here now, give us a kiss. I vow you will like it very much."

"In that you are very much mistaken," said a voice behind him, and before he had time to look around, a hand clamped down on his shoulder and spun him around and another hand slapped him resoundingly across the mouth.

Harry calmly took out his handkerchief and wiped his hand thoroughly. He then held out his arm for Sophia, who came to take it gratefully.

Charlie at this moment appeared in the doorway. He had seen Bruce take Sophia into the alcove, but as he was at that moment dancing with a young matron, it had taken him a bit longer to excuse himself and come to Sophia's rescue.

"What's to do here?" he enquired with a thunderous look at Bruce.

"Oh, Charlie, he—he—" began Sophia in a quavering voice, just barely holding back her tears.

"It's all right, Sophia. I will explain," said Harry soothingly, "Charlie, I believe Mr. Coverly will be taking his leave now, will you not, Mr. Coverly?" he inquired menacingly.

Bruce, still holding his hand to his mouth, which was bleeding slightly, looked up resentfully.

"I should like to know who you think you are, sir, to come bursting in here—"

"I am a guest of Mr. Portman's who would not dream of taking advantage of his hospitality by mauling his sister about. Now will you take yourself away, or shall you need my assistance to do so?" replied Harry, disengaging his arm from Sophia, and taking a step toward Bruce.

"Oh, very well, if you are going to behave in such a bullying way about it. It was all in fun, and if ever I saw a girl more eager—"

"Say another word, Coverly, and I shall be forced to come around tomorrow with my riding whip and teach you how to keep a civil tongue in your mouth," said Harry, now so angry he was white about the lips. Charles, his eyes flashing, moved forward and, taking Bruce's arm, jerked him up so that they were face to face, and spoke slowly, spacing his words out in a way that made Bruce cower away from him.

"Listen to me carefully, you despicable creature. You will leave this house immediately, and you will never be welcome here again. And if ever I hear one word of this episode from anyone, I will know you have spoken of it and I will make it my business to come and deal with you in a way you will not like at all. Now get out!"

He flung Bruce away from him, and Bruce turned sullenly and made his way out of the alcove. Charles followed him to make sure he was out of the house, and Harry calmly held out his arm to Sophia again.

"Come, my dear, shall we finish this dance?"

"Oh, Harry, that dreadful—dreadful man—" Sophia exclaimed, the tears of shame standing in her eyes.

"Now, Sophia, you are not to cry over anything such a fellow could say. You may be angry. In fact I would like to see you angry about it rather than tearful."

"All very well for you to say, Harry, but you were not the one to have those slimy hands all over you—" she began indignantly.

"There now, that is better. I told you that anger would deal better with the situation than tears," he said approvingly.

She had to laugh, albeit somewhat shakily, and taking his proffered handkerchief, dried her eyes. Then she took his arm and they went back to the dancing.

She was astonished to find that the party was going on gaily, and that no one had seemed to be aware of the little scene just enacted. She lifted her chin and smiled up at Harry. For once she seemed to have done something to please him. And the next dance, a waltz, was promised to Courtley. The evening was not ruined after all.

Chapter Nine

Sophia, that night, sat in front of her mirror, dreamily brushing her hair, while Augusta finished undressing, and Beth rushed about, hanging up gowns and putting away gloves and fans.

"Well, Sophia, you are looking uncommonly pleased with yourself," said Augusta, who had been observing her sister for a while.

"Oh, Gussie, was it not a lovely party? I will engage for it that it will turn out to be the most successful party of the Season."

"Well, it was fun, I give you that, but I could have done without several small annoyances," Augusta replied.

"And so could I," said Sophia, remembering with a shudder her encounter with Bruce Coverly. "Did—did you hear of what happened to me with that friend of Bramforth's?"

"Do you mean that spotty fellow, Bruce Coverly?"

"Yes, that one. He tried to—to—"

"Tried to kiss you!" said Augusta indignantly.

"Oh, Gussie, it was terrible. That awful mouth. I thought I should faint."

"Faint! I should have boxed his ears, let me tell you, if he had tried it with me. How did you—where—?"

"Well, I was trying to get away from him. He kept saying such awful things when we were dancing. I said I was too warm and before I knew what was happening he had taken me into the alcove. I immediately got up and tried to leave, but then he grabbed me and—oh, I cannot even bear to tell you of it, it was so awful."

"Did he actually kiss you?"

"Well, no, because just then Harry came in and slapped him and told him to leave and then Charlie came and took him away."

"Good. I wish I had been there to see it. Do you know who he is, Soph?"

"Why, Bruce Coverly, you said, a friend of Bramforth Wixton's."

"Yes, and a brother to the terrible Letitia!"

"Letitia! Good heavens! Well, that explains everything, for a more disagreeable girl I never met in my life than Letitia. Just think, Gussie, we very nearly had her for a sister-in-law instead of our darling Mallory!"

"It doesn't bear thinking of. Well, we both had our trials tonight, dear Soph. I must admit, mine was not so hard to bear as yours. Still, Bramforth Wixton is very trying."

"Do you know, Gussie," said Sophia, changing the subject, "I believe I succeeding in pleasing Harry tonight, for a change."

Augusta looked at her, her heart sinking, but with a brave smile asked her to explain and then congratulated her on her behavior. She told herself that she had no right to feel depressed. Harry had been Sophia's from the beginning, and she, Gussie, had only herself to blame if she had let herself indulge in feelings for him that she had no right to have. She told herself that this was but a passing fancy, that London was filled with charming men, and before the season was over she would be sure to meet at least one who appealed to her as much as Harry did. Never, never, would she betray her feelings to Sophia. If Sophia was now falling in love with Harry, then she should have him, and have him without any feelings of guilt that she was making her sister unhappy. Augusta got into bed and thumped her pillow angrily. *And that's the end of the matter,* she told herself firmly.

Sophia said good night and turned over to fall asleep thinking of how blissful it was to waltz with Courtley, and how good it had felt to see Harry looking at her approvingly for a change.

When Bramforth left the party, he found Bruce skulking about in the street, waiting for him to come out.

"Here, where did you get to, Coverly? I looked all over for you," said Bram, as they walked off down the street together.

"Damned tiresome affair. Couldn't be bothered to stay," said Bruce sullenly.

"Oh, my dear fellow, how can you say so? Thought it charming myself. Though I'll be damned if I understand women. Here I am making all sorts of a fool of myself over Miss Portman, and can't seem to get anywhere."

"Waste of time, Bram, waste of time. Much better-looking women than that about," was Bruce's disagreeable reply.

"Oh, coming it a bit too strong. Beautiful girl. And a very handsome dowry goes with her too. Certainly a very worthwhile project, I'd say."

"Don't like the family. You know that Portman jilted my sister, don't you?"

"Now that's a clanker if ever I heard one. The shoe on the other foot, from all that I heard about it."

"Well, you heard wrong," Bruce said truculently.

"All right, all right, no need to fly into the boughs. Look here, Coverly, you've had plenty of experience with the fair sex. What line do you think I should take with the Portman wench, eh?"

"Rough," growled Bruce spitefully. "All women like rough treatment best, no matter how they behave."

"Do you think so? Hmmm. Well, I must give that some thought, I suppose."

They walked off into the night, looking for an inn where drink stronger than ratafia and lemonade could be found.

Mallory's maid had helped her to remove her silvery gray ball gown and hung it away. Seated now in front of her mirror while her hair was being brushed, Mallory reflected upon the success of her party. All her guests had congratulated her as they left on a most delightful time, and they had all seemed gay and happy at the end of the evening.

A knock at her door announced the arrival of her husband, and Mallory called for him to come in.

He settled into an armchair next to her dressing table to watch her hair being brushed, one of his favorite occupations. The long rippling black waves crackled and sparked with life under the vigorously wielded brush.

"I think everything went very well, don't you Charles?"

"I would say so," replied Charles carefully, eyeing the maid and then deciding it would be better to hold his tongue until she was out of the room. She was a most loyal girl, but servants *did* gossip. Not that he blamed them much. The lives of their master and mistress became their lives, and added, for them, the color and excitement their own did not provide.

"The girls were certainly never lacking a partner. I think perhaps Sophia danced too many times with Courtley. Of course, they are childhood friends and we make little of it, but others noticed, I believe."

"Pooh, everyone knows they are old friends and think nothing of it."

"Well, it seemed to me that Harry was not so pleased."

"Harry? Danced with her more than once himself, if it comes to that. I imagine that raised more eyebrows than Courtley."

"Well, but I still think Harry does not like it. I should not, in his place."

"Now don't go jumping the gun, my dear. Not a word

has been said so far, not even an indication of how he feels, other than his obvious attraction."

"But, Charles, I'm sure he is in love with her."

"Well, he's said nothing to me, and I'm sure I will hear from him when his mind is made up."

"Just think what a brilliant match for Sophia. Why, he is the catch of the Season!"

Charlie watched his wife's excited face in the mirror and had to smile at her enthusiasm. She cared so much for the girls, and wanted so much for them. He only hoped Harry was right for Sophia. He had had some suspicions that all might not be as easy as Mallory thought, and was a bit surprised that she had not felt it also. But then, she *had* expressed something of what he was feeling, when she mentioned Courtley. It might turn out that they had both taken Courtley too much for granted.

Mallory finally dismissed her maid, and turned to hold out her hands to Charles.

"Now, out with it. What is it you haven't told me?"

Charles laughed. "Am I so easy to read as all that?"

"To me you are, thank heaven. I should hate to think we were so far apart that I could not tell when something was bothering you."

"Ah, my love, my little love." He held her close and for a few moments whatever was bothering Charles ceased to matter to either of them. But finally she pushed him away and demanded an explanation. He told her of the episode in the alcove with Sophia and Bruce Coverly.

As he recounted the ugly story, Mallory's cheeks flamed with angry color and her lips were pressed into a thin line.

"That little—monster!' she burst out. When he was finished, she cried, "That disgusting scoundrel! That he should come into our house uninvited and behave so! How *dare* he put his hands on Sophia?"

"Now, now." He soothed her. "It's all over, and though it was most unpleasant, I don't think Sophia came to any real harm. It may well have been good for her."

"Good for her! How can you say so? Surely no girl can benefit from such insulting behavior."

"Well, Sophia is much too trusting and—soft. She needs to be toughened up a bit, make more of a demand on herself. She's fine when she's with Augusta, borrows some of Gussie's spirit, but on her own she lets people walk all over her for fear of hurting their feelings."

"But surely it is not a bad thing to be sensitive and sympathetic to the feelings of others? After all, that is the mark of a true gentlewoman."

"Well, I think Gussie is sensitive too, but she is also sensitive for herself, and doesn't want to be trampled upon."

"Yes," she answered thoughtfully. Then: "Charles, do you think Gussie is quite—happy?"

"Why, of course she is. Now, what maggot have you got in your brain?"

"I can't say, quite. But recently it seems to me that when she thinks no one is observing her, she gets a sort of sad look in her eyes."

"And I think my sweet wife is letting her imagination run astray. You think you have Sophia practically settled, and won't rest until you have Gussie fixed also. Meantime, you need something to fret over."

"Oh, Charles," she protested laughingly, "surely I never fret."

"Now and then you do. But do you put the twins' problems out of your mind. They are grown-up young ladies, very well trained by yourself and will get along just fine alone. Besides, soon you will have something else to fret over, something that will be much more demanding than those girls."

"Yes," she said with a sigh of great contentment, nuzzling her face against the silk of his dressing gown. "I shall have indeed."

The Duchess of Carnmoor, having spent a satisfactory evening at whist with Mrs. Wixton, was in her bed, waiting patiently, but not too hopefully, for sleep to come. Strange, she thought, how much less sleep one requires as one grows older. She changed her position slightly to ease a rheumatic knee, and thought about her son and the

Portman girl. It would be a most satisfactory arrangement, she thought, for the Portmans were a fine old family with a great deal of money. Not that that mattered, the money, the Lord knew Harry had more than enough of his own. *Most importantly, I like the girl,* she thought to herself with a smile. She realized that she presented a doughty picture. In fact she deliberately played the part to make up to herself for growing old and losing her looks. *Ah,* she thought to herself with satisfaction, *I was a beautiful girl!*

Her mind flitted among images of herself in white satin hoops with cherry-striped panels and a towering white wig at Court; of herself surrounded by admiring men at a ball; of a certain walk in the moonlight with Carnmoor. Now there was a man! Arrogant, proud and handsome, but oh, the sweetness. And how good he had been to her, and she such a flighty, willful thing. But Carnmoor had adored her spirit. Harry was exactly like his father, and it seemed to her strange that Harry should not seek the same thing in a wife as his father had.

Carnmoor would have gone for the other one, Augusta Portman. *Now there is a girl very much as I was myself,* she thought. *Plenty of gumption there. She'd give Harry a run for his money, I'll be bound. I fear very much that he is too strong for Sophia. He'll walk all over her and she will end up being miserable and he bored.*

Mrs. Wixton's voice came into her mind, telling her of Bramforth's *tendre* for Miss Portman, and with many sly looks and winks and smiles, intimating that there might soon be very good news from that direction. *Pah!* thought the duchess, *as if that girl would ever look twice at that puffing, dough-faced son of Amabel Wixton's.* Of course, one knew that Amabel was wild to find an heiress for her son, but to send him snuffling after a beautiful girl like Augusta Portman showed a lack of wit on Amabel's part, which the duchess would never have credited if she hadn't heard it. And what had he to offer such a girl? Obesity, a huge appetite, stupidity and a complete want of address, not to mention the fact that he was penniless! Really, how was it possible for some mothers to be so blind about their children?

She thought of Harry proudly, now there was a son a mother could look upon without shame, and could be assured that any girl he decided upon would feel honored to be so chosen. One didn't see the Portman girls turning away from *her* son. In fact both girls looked at him with that certain light in their eyes, if she was any judge, But evidently Harry was not aware of it.

Ah well, she sighed, and turned over. *Harry must be allowed to have his own tastes, after all, and perhaps he feels he has all the temperament he wants in one family.* She wondered if she should give a small dinner party for the Portmans, to introduce her friends to the girl. On the other hand, she would have to think about it. It might be too soon.

Chapter Ten

A few evenings later Mallory led the way into the rooms
at Almack's, and was received most graciously by the
forbidding Lady Jersey. Mallory's mother, as well as
the twins' mother, had been great friends with this lady
many years before, so the Portman women were always
very sure of being approved of by the powerful patronesses
of Almacks. The Portmans went at least once a week
during the Season, and always enjoyed themselves im-
mensely. Charles accompanied them on occasion, but had
begged off this evening, claiming to have had enough
dancing after Mallory's party to last him for awhile.

The girls after making their curtseys, were swept up by
friends, and immediately became the center of a chattering
group of young ladies, all twittering and fluttering and
exclaiming over each other's gowns.

Augusta, in pale orange creped muslin opening over
white satin, and Sophia in apple-green gauze were, to
Mallory, the most beautiful girls in the room, and she

watched the slow drift of gentlemen, crossing the room to greet them, with a triumphant gleam in her eye.

Harry appeared, and without seeming in any way to be rude, managed to get through the crowd and extract Sophia with no trouble at all. Mallory noted Augusta turning to look after them for an instant, and in that brief flash, thought she saw again that small dimming of sadness. But there, perhaps Charles was right, and she was only creating something to fret over. Now she saw Augusta turn to greet Courtley, who was introducing her to a tall, handsome gentleman, who shortly afterwards led her off to the dance floor. He must have been a most amusing fellow, thought Mallory, for she could see Augusta laughing more than once. When the dance was finished, he led her off, and there waiting for her, was Bramforth Wixton. Mallory saw Augusta draw back and then be forced to politely stand and listen. She seemed to give a negative answer and then apparently decided that politeness would not allow her to be rude, and she took Bramforth's arm and was again led to the floor.

Augusta had indeed given Bram a negative answer when he had presented himself and asked if she would do him the honor of giving him the next dance.

"Why, thank you, Mr. Wixton, but I had thought to sit awhile."

"Wonderful, Miss Portman. Nothing I would enjoy more. Indeed, I prefer a quiet tête-à-tête to the dance. Much more chance of carrying on an—interesting conversation." He leered at her suggestively.

Augusta changed her mind instantly at the picture of herself in intimate conversation again with Bramforth, and told him she thought she would dance after all.

"Ah well, then I must content myself, Miss Portman. Whatever will give you pleasure will pleasure me. You have so captured my mind that I can think only of being of service to you."

Several extremely apropos retorts occurred to Augusta in response to this, but she contented herself by replying, "I assure you you have no cause to so exercise yourself, Mr. Wixton. It is not necessary in the least. On the contrary, to give you the truth with no bark on it, it is a complete waste of your time."

"Oh, do not say so, Miss Portman, I beg you. It could never be a waste of time for *me*," he persisted, with his version of a gay little laugh, to indicate that he was being flirtatious. He really felt in fine fettle. Not hearing the boredom and contempt in her voice, he assumed their conversation to be light-hearted banter.

Augusta mentally shrugged and made no answer, for, indeed, she felt there was no point in continuing. The Wixtons must inherit their thick skins with the name, she thought, for Mrs. Wixton had the same talent for not hearing what the other person said and plowed on as blindly with her own thoughts.

When the dance finished Bramforth led her to a seat and prepared to sit beside her and continue his flirtation. But first Courtley, then Harry, saw her plight and presented themselves for her rescue. Some perversity made her give her hand to Courtley, much as she would have preferred to dance with Harry. *No,* she thought, *not perversity, but only following my new policy. I will not be cold to him, but simply—indifferent.* She watched Harry cross to Sophia and hold out his hand, and she saw how Sophia seemed to smile up at him so eagerly. *So,* she thought, *I am right and she is falling in love with him.* Augusta threw back her head and gave Courtley such a dazzling smile that he frowned for a moment, wondering what could be the matter with her. He was not used to receiving such looks from Augusta.

"Why are you acting like that, Gussie?"

The smile disappeared. "Acting like what?" she asked crossly.

"Well, I don't know, like Letitia Coverly used to act, oh so belle-of-the-ballish, if you know what I mean."

"Don't be nonsensical, Courtley. I simply smiled because I was happy to be rescued from that dreadful bore, Bramforth Wixton. It was happy relief."

"Looked more 'I'll show them all,' " said Courtley with startling insight. Augusta gaped at him for a moment, and then smiled her usual warm smile, and squeezed his hand in a friendly way.

"How did you like my friend, Hampton Madderson?" he asked, now that she was behaving like the Gussie he had always known.

"Oh, very pleasant, Courtley. A great deal of wit also, which makes things easier," she replied enthusiastically.

"I thought he was your style," he said with an air of self-congratulation.

"Oh yes, I set a great deal of store by wit," she answered. "It can compensate for all sorts of inadequacies."

"What sorts?"

"Oh, looks, polish, grace. All those things that are attractive on the surface, but can become boring without wit."

"Augusta, you are formidable, you quite frighten me!"

"Pooh, I will engage for it that you have more wit than most people in this room."

"I don't know that I can accept that as a compliment when I see such people as Bramforth Wixton skulking about."

"Where? Oh, Courtley, I beg of you, do not take me off the floor in his direction," she requested, with a quick darting look about the room.

Courtley laughed, "No fear. I've already sworn to Hampton to lead you directly to him. I hope you are not promised for the next dance, for he is determined."

"No, I am not, and I shall be quite content with Mr. Madderson."

Courtley was glad to see her face brighten at the thought of his friend. He was very fond of Hampton and pleased to know that two of his good friends should think kindly of each other. Courtley himself was feeling less than happy these days. His feelings for Sophia had grown from youthful infatuation to real love, and his heart was very sore to see her evident preference for Carnmoor. Courtley had never declared himself, believing it was not fair to do so before she had had a chance to become acquainted with other young men. He now thought he might have been too sanguine about his own prospects, had assumed too much on their old friendship. And really, he could not blame any woman for preferring Carnmoor to himself. Harry was a duke, after all, fabulously wealthy, and handsome besides. *Why, I like him very much myself. He really is a capital fellow,* thought Courtley. But just the same, Courtley was unhappy.

However, he did not show this to Augusta, but smiling broadly, led her off, directly up to his friend, Hampton.

"You see how well I strive to please you, Hampton. Here is Miss Portman, delivered into your hands."

"You are a grand fellow, Courtley. Miss Portman, I hope you will understand and forgive our little conspiracy," replied Hampton, bowing to Augusta.

"Surely no lady could take offense at such a flattering situation, sir?"

"You are kind as well as beautiful, Miss Portman. Will you do me the honor?" he asked, holding out his arm.

"With pleasure, Mr. Madderson," she answered.

But her mind was with Courtley. She had seen the unhappiness in his eyes, whether he would have her or no, and she couldn't help reflecting on the tangled state of all their lives at this point. The only uncertainty was Sophia herself, whose preference Augusta still could not discover.

Hampton, when the figure of the dance brought them together, contented himself with watching her face, which he found altogether enchanting.

She finally became aware of her rudeness and of his close regard, and blushed slightly.

"I beg your pardon, Mr. Madderson. I'm afraid my mind was wandering," she said apologeticaly.

"I was most happily occupied, Miss Portman."

She dimpled prettily. "Now, that was gracious, Mr. Madderson."

"No trouble at all, Miss Portman, happy to oblige you at any time. When I have the proper inspiration I am able to do it quite easily."

"I'm sure you are able to do it quite easily in any case, Mr. Madderson."

"Ah, now you hurt me, Miss Portman, by implying that I am but an amusing rattle."

"Oh, no, not a rattle, amusing certainly, and that, believe me, is no small commodity."

"Well, I must console myself with that thought, I suppose. I have heard that you are becoming quite an expert whip."

"Oh, far from expert. Carnmoor is teaching me what he can. Now *he* is an expert. He drives so—easily, it makes me feel quite ham-fisted."

"Your hands could never have that appellation, Miss Portman," he said, drawing up to his lips the hand he was at that moment holding, to kiss it lightly.

Augusta could not help finding this gallantry and his very obvious interest gratifying in the extreme. It soothed her aching heart to a degree she would not have believed possible, and she smiled warmly up at him in response.

Decorum would not allow him to dance with her any further during the evening, for that would have made her the object of unnecessary gossip, and the possible disapproval of the forbidding patronesses. But he did contrive to request the pleasure of taking her riding the next day, which she happily granted.

During the rest of the evening she was fortunate to be always promised when Bramforth succeeded in getting close to her, and managed to enjoy herself. But she hated the feeling of someone unpleasant waiting always to pounce in an unguarded moment. She wondered if she should have Charlie speak to him.

Sophia danced more than twice with Harry, and since rumors of their impending engagement were rife, this conduct was looked upon indulgently by the chaperones.

Harry had been charming to her all evening, never getting his impatient look, and complimenting her on her gown and her dancing. She had relaxed under this treatment, and laughed and chatted with him easily. *Really,* she thought, *he is a delightful man and I do like him very much.*

She confided as much to Mallory, as they sat together between dances. Mallory smiled knowingly.

"I felt sure you would come to feel that way, Sophia.

Indeed, I don't see how you could help yourself. He is such a dear, he reminds me of Charles."

"He does?" asked Sophia wonderingly. "Why, yes, I suppose they are like in some ways."

"Oh, yes. That lovely warmth and humor. I have always thought so."

"I think you are right, Mallory. I guess I never thought of it that way."

But now that she *did* think of it, she wondered that she had never seen what was obvious to others from the beginning. Everyone liked him so well, and were so congratulatory in their attitude toward her for having captured him, that she wondered at it that she had taken so long. They were right. It was a wonderful thing to have the devotion of a man like Harry. Her feelings for Courtley were those of a child who had no other friends and clung to the first one because it was safe and comfortable. Perhaps "love" was this disturbed discomfort she experienced generally with Harry. And besides, it was a bit too late to think of discouraging him now, after having allowed him to behave in a distinctly loverlike fashion, and being accepted as such by all of society. It would be a shameful thing to turn away from him after having encouraged him so far. He would be so hurt, poor fellow, so humiliated. *No, no,* she thought hastily, *I will never behave in so rag-mannered a way*.

Harry, looking down at Sophia's sweet, beautiful face as they danced, called himself every kind of fool to have allowed the situation to go so far without discovering the true state of his feelings. That he actually was in love with Augusta was surely a disastrous state of affairs. This revelation had not come to him in a blinding flash, but had grown steadily during their sessions alone when he was teaching her to drive. Her courage and mind were unequaled by any woman he had ever met, with the possible exception of his mother. And that she was an exact copy in looks of this lovely creature he was dancing with was even more astounding, for it was Sophia's beauty that had captured his imagination before he had come to know either sister.

He thought, as Augusta had, upon the tangle they were in. For there was that charming fellow, Armstead, in love with Sophia, and he himself in love with Augusta, and if he had not mistaken it, he could swear there was an answering response from Augusta toward him, when he caught her eye in an unguarded moment. But now it was too late. He could never allow it to be said that a Carn-moor would lead a girl on and then drop her, after arousing her expectations. He could never behave so shabbily. There was nothing for it. He must soon make his proposal to Sophia. He decided he would speak to his mother about it at the first opportunity.

Chapter Eleven

The trees along the path, in their new green spring clothes, threw only the slightest dappled shade over the early morning riders in the park. Augusta and Hampton rode along quietly together, in the sweet air filled with only the sound of their horse's hooves and the business of birds getting on with their nest-building and breakfast-finding.

Augusta marveled at the companionable silence between them. This man seemed to sense her mood and be content to join her in it, showing an unusual sensitivity as far as Augusta was concerned.

Presently she broke the silence to inquire about his acquaintance with Courtley.

"Oh, we've met in London from time to time over the years. He's a very pleasant person to be friends with, I've found, and now I've discovered it is also profitable."

"Profitable? You are in business together?"

He laughed, "No. I meant that he has added considerably to my happiness by making me acquainted with a most beautiful lady."

"I thank you, sir. I make no doubt Courtley has told you of how we are acquainted." At his nod, she continued. "He was our first friend, though he must have thought us shocking at first sight. We ran wild down in the country before Mallory took us in hand, barefoot most of the time and hair unbrushed. But Courtley took it all in his stride. He and Sophia were always very close."

"I think that is so even today," he said tentatively.

"Yes, I'm afraid it is," she replied with a tiny frown. "I feel there might be some unhappiness in store for dear Courtley."

"Yes. I had noticed—certain things that lead me to feel it might be so."

Neither felt willing to explore this avenue any further, and they rode along silently for awhile.

"Do you make your home in London, Mr. Madderson?"

"Yes, with my mother. We have a home in Devon, but rarely go there these days. My mother is quite crippled with rheumatism, and says if she must be confined she would much rather be in London than in the wilds of Devon. She entertains a steady stream of cronies, plays whist continuously, and leads me around by the nose!"

"That must be difficult from her chair," Augusta laughed.

"Oh, that is not the least of her handicaps. She is but a tiny thing. Barely reaches my shoulder, but she accomplishes her tyranny with an astonishing ease."

"You break my heart, sir. The picture of such a great creature as yourself being so treated is such a sad one."

"I knew I could win your sympathy, Miss Portman, if I but presented myself as a pitiful soul, nagged to death and in need of help."

"You require rescue from this dragon? A St. George on a white charger?" she quipped.

"Well—perhaps a St. Georgina, if you don't mind. I think you just might be a match for my mother."

Augusta laughed. "I seem ever to find myself in a joust with someone's mother, and generally the someone is a gentleman. I shall soon have a most unusual reputation amongst the dowagers of London."

"You would be equal even to that, I'm sure, Miss Portman. If your sister is anything like you, you must be a formidable pair," he said.

"Oh, did you not meet Sophia? She is not like me at all, except in looks. She is the well-behaved half."

"It is often so with twins, I have been told, that one will be quiet and more timid, while the other is more—more—"

"Loud and pushing?" she teased.

"Not in the least," he replied calmly. "More witty and high-spirited."

"There! As nice a bit of compliment-fishing as I have been guilty of in many weeks. And you took the bait very well."

"Miss Portman," he said gravely, "I cannot allow you to allude to me as being fishlike."

Augusta gurgled. "Oh dear, now I have been most ungracious, returning a compliment with a slur. Say you forgive me, Mr. Madderson, or my morning will be quite ruined."

"It would make me happy to think that I was capable of ruining your morning," he responded.

"Why, Mr. Madderson, what a thing to say!"

"I assure you I meant it in the most complimentary way."

"Explain yourself," she said sternly.

"Why, only that it would please me to think that anything I could or could not do would have an effect upon you, Miss Portman," he said with a smile, but in entire seriousness.

Augusta, struck by that seriousness, found herself lowering her eyes in some confusion, and hoping desperately that she would not blush. Her reaction to his compliment took her by surprise. She was not immodest, but she had had more than her fair share of praises from gentlemen in her two seasons, and felt she had enough intelligence to know them for what they were usually—certainly well enough not to take them seriously. They were part of the game played by ladies and gentlemen of fashion, one that she had always rather enjoyed.

Now, for some reason, she felt that she was being less than fair with this very nice man, to allow this note of seriousness to continue. How if she said to him, "Sir, much as I feel that we might indeed suit very well, it is too late. My heart has been given"?

On the other hand, did she really consider herself as on the shelf for the rest of her life, because she had had the misfortune to fall in love with her sister's beau? Was she truly so romantical that she was considering pining away like some heroine of a tragedy? She had to pooh-pooh such a notion, for she knew herself well enough to know that she was not cut out for tragedy, or for heroism either, come to that. She would soon tire of such a pose, and brush it impatiently aside to get on with life.

Well then, she thought, *so what is all of this about? Here you are with an extremely handsome man who is everything you could want in a beau for yourself, and you are striking these attitudes!* She had to laugh at herself, and without realizing it, did so aloud.

"Well, Miss Portman, I am glad that you have finally decided to be amused by my compliment. I had not meant for it to amuse you, but for a moment there I was afraid I had offended you."

"I'm sure I beg your pardon, Mr. Madderson. That was very rude of me, but I sometimes do allow my mind to go off on its own in that way, a dreadful habit. Of course I was not offended. In fact, I was so pleased that I was trying to remember when last I heard such a nice thing said to me."

"Now that is a Banbury tale, if I ever heard one," he said, "for if ever I've met a woman who I felt sure received compliments continuously, you are the one."

"Ah, but not given to me in such a way that it required an explanation from the giver for me to understand it."

They looked at each other, and Hampton held out his hand and she laid her own in it for a brief moment. Then they laughed together very happily and rode on quite in charity with one another.

But the moment had not been so brief that it was not seen. Several people saw it and took note and were either glad or perturbed, as it affected their own cases.

Harry, cantering along with Sophia on the other side of the road, had seen them from some distance away, and while idly answering Sophia who had not yet seen them, had watched the entire vignette. *Well,* he thought, *and what did I expect? That she would not fall in love someday?*

In her carriage behind them, unbeknownst to Augusta, was the Duchess of Carnmoor, taking the air with her friend, Mrs. Wixton. They had both been witnesses to the scene. The duchess, seeing Harry coming down the road with one twin, had realized the girl ahead of her must be Augusta, and thought no more about it, except that they were both fine horsewomen.

However, Mrs. Wixton could not view the situation with such dispassion. Here was Bramforth's—well, not exactly his fiancée, but very nearly, to Mrs. Wixton's mind, laughing and flirting and holding hands right in public view with another man. Mrs. Wixton seethed, and finally, unable to restrain herself, burst out.

"*Who* can that be with Augusta Portman? And how dare he hold her hand like that? What can she mean by letting him?"

The duchess looked at her shrewdly, guessing what was bothering her. "Why, Amabel, he looks a very pleasant sort of fellow, to be sure. And they did no more than shake hands, as friends often do in agreement over something."

"Hmpff," sniffed Mrs. Wixton. "It looked a great deal more than that to me."

"But Amabel," said the duchess, somewhat slyly, "why should you mind so much? It was nothing so very objectionable, after all."

"Well, I'm sure I don't know what Bramforth would think if he had seen it," snapped Mrs. Wixton.

"But why should Bramforth have anything to say to it?"

Mrs. Wixton hesitated, wondering if she should confide in her friend or not. But finally her tongue overcame her caution.

"Oh, Margaret, dear Bramforth has finally fallen in love," she rhapsodized, clasping her hands and smiling gaily. "I have not wanted to say a word too soon, but you know how I have longed for him to be married and have a family. I've always wanted a daughter, as well you know, and darling grandchildren, but I had quite despaired of Bramforth's ever finding someone who would suit him. He is so sensitive, you know. And now—now it seems all my dreams are to be fulfilled. From the moment he saw Miss Portman—well, there was no holding him back. He must have her, he declared, and he has confided to me that she has not found his attentions unwelcome."

The duchess listened to this girlish gushing, with such a look of disbelief in her face that had Mrs. Wixton been aware of it she would have been quite dashed. But Mrs. Wixton was rarely open to nuance, even in speech.

"Amabel, I'm sure I wish you to be happy in every way, but I think you may be anticipating just a little bit, don't you? I can't help feeling that they would not suit. Miss Portman is so volatile and Bramforth is—well—"

"Yes, I know, he is a very gentle soul. But opposite characters are drawn to each other, don't you see? I feel sure she must feel soothed by the quiet and solidity of a personality like Bramforth's. And I'm sure that marriage and a family will calm her volatility. Oh, I admire it in a young girl, don't misunderstand me. And so does Bramforth. He was immediately captured by it, but it can be unbecoming in a married woman."

The duchess, being used to the folly of nearly everyone she encountered, was rather amused than outraged by Mrs. Wixton's pretensions. She knew full well that a girl like Augusta Portman could never be attracted to a man like Bramforth Wixton, and if by some impossible to imagine chance that she should be, her family would never allow her to marry a penniless nobody. That this should not also be apparent to Mrs. Wixton was no surprise to her, for well she knew that people saw only what they wanted to see, and believed only what they wanted to believe.

Yet another person had been on the scene while it was being played out. Bruce Coverly, cantering along looking about for an acquaintance with whom to scrape up some conversation, had seen. But since he was several places behind Harry and Sophia and had not seen them, he assumed the girl to be Sophia, and raged inwardly that she would let the whole world see her holding hands with one man, and yet behave like a squeamish miss barely out of the schoolroom when she was with him.

Damned little hussy, he thought savagely, *no better than she should be, I'll be bound,* and decided forthwith to ride round to his club and tell this story, with perhaps an embellishment here and there to spice it up. *Serve her right to have her name being bandied about, serve them all right, all of those Portmans, too damned high in the instep. Do them good to have a setdown.*

Naturally, the first person he encountered when he reached his club should be Bramforth, and he told his story with relish, making it seem that he had been witness to a lover's tryst, no less, and that a great deal besides a brief handclasp had occurred.

Bram was not overly excited by this tale. He was never very interested in anything that did not concern him directly. It was too tiring, he found. But he did make mention of it to his mother when he reached home for luncheon.

Mrs. Wixton, still churning with indignation when she had reached home, had finally managed to calm herself. After all, it was but a small thing, as dear Margaret said, and it would not do to get Bramforth upset, or in any way to turn him against the girl when all was going so well.

Now, hearing Bramforth mention it, but that it had been Sophia, she was of two minds. The terrible need to set things straight, to impart the "real" information, a trait of the true gossip, almost overcame her discretion. And then again, it might be a good thing to tell him so that he could just drop a word in Augusta's ear that he had heard of it. Yes, that might be the best way.

"Bram, dear, actually it was Miss Portman, not Miss Sophia. Miss Sophia was riding with Harry. I don't know the gentleman Miss Portman was with, but since we were directly behind them, I can tell you that your informant was entirely wrong. It was a mere handshake. Even the duchess said so, nothing to get upset about."

"Miss Portman?" His eyes opened a little wider than was their wont. "Well, I think I must just speak to her of this, all the same," he said portentously. "Won't do to have her behaving that way and having people talk of her, even if the duchess does say it was nothing. After all, Coverly saw it quite differently, and so may others."

"You may be right, Bramforth. Have you—spoken to her—seriously, I mean?"

"Oh, not to say out and out, no. But I've no doubt she has understood my feelings."

"It never does to take these things for granted with a girl, Bramforth. Women, alas, are not free to express their feelings until the gentleman has spoken, you see. It might be just as well to fix your interests with her as soon as possible."

"Never does to rush these things, Mama. All in good time, all in good time," said Bram, unwilling, as always, to exert himself if there was some way to escape it.

"Bramforth! Miss Portman is a very popular young lady, seen everywhere, and no doubt has already received several proposals. For instance, the gentleman she was with today was very handsome indeed, and extremely well-dressed. I make no doubt there is money there. Silly, really, to let such a prize slip through your fingers from lack of enterprise."

Bram considered this for a moment, and then shrugged his shoulders irritably.

"Oh, very well, Mama, very well. Might as well get it over with, I suppose, and be done with it. I'll just drop around and pop the question."

Chapter Twelve

The duchess stabbed her needle through the center of a flower on her embroidery frame and looked up at Harry, who was beginning to irritate her. However, she spoke mildly.

"Harry, if you kick that log again you will quite destroy the fire."

"What's that? Oh, sorry." He left off kicking, but continued to stand there gazing abstractly into the flames.

"Something worrying you, my dear?"

"Oh no, not to say worrying. Just trying to make up my mind about something."

"Can I be of help?"

"Thank you," he said with a smile at her, "but I believe I've come to the only decision I can make. Mama, you *do* like Sophia, do you not?"

"Very lovely girl," responded the duchess promptly.

"I am very glad to hear you say so, for I plan to ask her to be my wife."

"Ah."

" 'Ah'? Now what can you mean by that?" he asked.

"I mean nothing at all. I am very happy for you, dear Harry, as well you know, and I shall be very happy to welcome your wife to our family."

He continued to stare at her quizzically. He knew his mother well enough to know that there was some thought, some comment, being withheld. He had a fairly good idea of what it was, for he also knew that his mother was as well acquainted with him as he with her. No doubt she had realized there was some ambivalence in his feelings about Sophia. Whether she had reached the correct conclusions about the true state of his emotions regarding Augusta he could not know. However, he was sure that she had realized that there was only one honorable course that he could take, after having pursued Sophia so openly in the beginning. All of their circle of acquaintance were now in daily expectation of an announcement, and it must certainly be true that Sophia herself must be waiting for him to speak.

He did love Sophia in a mild, protective way, and he made no doubt that in time, that feeling would grow, and that they could make a good life together. The wild, passionate love he felt for Augusta, he had firmly sealed over in his heart this morning when he had seen her give her hand and her heart-stopping smile to Hampton Madderson.

What we shared, he thought, *may have only been felt by me . . . the certainty I had that we were sharing the same feelings only a product of wishful thinking.*

But surely I couldn't have felt that rightness if she were not experiencing it also, his heart protested.

There, enough. I will not think of this any more, he told himself firmly. But the thoughts continued despite this injunction. *For what if she* had *felt it,* they pursued, *what would you do? Go to Sophia and say, "I'm sorry, my dear, but I find I have made a mistake, and it is Augusta who will suit me best"? A fine sort of person that would make me.*

"I shall have a dinner party to introduce her to everyone officially," declared the duchess, interrupting his thoughts.

"That will be very kind of you," he responded, stepping over to her and kissing her withered cheek with great love in his heart for her. "I will tell her of it. Best go and get it over with now, I think."

As she watched him go out the door she felt her heart ache for him. It was a not joyous thing, as it should be, and she wished there were some way she could make it so for him, as mothers all feel. But as they also know, children must always work these things out for themselves. He had changed his mind, that much she knew, but had realized things had now gone too far to back out honorably. It would be best if the girl herself refused him, but there was little hope of that, the duchess felt sure. She could not imagine a girl refusing Harry.

When Harry arrived at the Portmans' to make his proposal, every member of the household was perfectly aware of his purpose. The butler, who showed him into the drawing room to Mallory, made haste to spread the word in the servants' quarters. Mallory, after greeting him, hurried away to fetch Sophia, and then to find Charlie in his library and give him the news. Fortunately, Augusta had gone with Jane and Lady Tilden to inspect the wares at a silk warehouse.

Beth, trying to unfasten the back of Sophia's dress, was so overcome with excitement she could hardly make her fingers work.

"Oh, Miss, 'ee'll wear your primrose, a picture 'ee'll be. Ah, so fine a man, and a duke! Not that 'ee don't deserve a duke, and I'd like to hear anyone say else. Draw 'is cork for 'im, I would," she declared stoutly.

Sophia looked shocked. "Beth, wherever did you hear such a vulgar expression? I can see London is not good for you."

"Never 'ee mind, Missie. Mayhap I be good for London. Show 'em what kind of backbones we got in the country, even if we ain't up to scratch on posh city ways."

Beth peeled the dress down and whipped the primrose

lawn over Sophia's head and settled it into place expertly.

"Now, don't 'ee be nervous, Miss Sophia. You be just such a good country girl as I be, for all you're quality. And as good as a duke any day. Think on Miss Augusta. She'd not be shy, not 'er. Give 'em as good as she gets, she does."

Sophia laughed, though a bit wistfully. She knew how well dear Gussie would handle this situation, and wished Gussie were here at this moment to help her get through it. Sophia's stomach had been behaving in a most erratic way ever since Mallory had come to tell her that Harry wished to speak with her in the drawing room. Mallory had hugged and kissed Sophia, and then smiling broadly, hurried away. It was then the strange fluttery sensation had begun.

Unlike most girls, and certainly unlike Gussie, Sophia did not crave excitement or suspense in her life. Her sunny and undemanding disposition needed only to know that those around her were happy and she was content. Therefore, she was not enjoying the turbulence of her feelings at this moment. She felt silly and trembly, neither of which sensations were pleasurable. Added to this was a barely acknowledged reluctance, and a most unaccountable sadness.

She tried, as Beth finished fastening her dress and then began to brush her hair, to talk herself out of this strange reluctance to hear Harry's declaration. *It is only that it is my first proposal,* she told herself, *and every young girl must feel just so the first time.* She tried to imagine what he would say and how she would respond: calm and serene? No, she knew she would never be able to manage such a demeanor with Harry.

Oh dear, she thought, *love is not nearly so enjoyable as I had always thought it would be. It's too—too—uncomfortable to enjoy.*

When she presented herself in the drawing room, she behaved, as she had somehow known was inevitable, with the sort of simpering and blushing Gussie so deplored in her. She tried desperately to raise her eyes and look at Harry without success.

"Sophia, my dear," said Harry, coming to her and taking her hand. "How very beautiful you are looking today."

"Th-th-thank you, Harry. Is it not a lovely day?"

"Yes, it is indeed," he lead her to a sofa and she sat down with him beside her. "Sophia, I have not gone through the formality of speaking to Charlie yet, for permission to address you. You know how much I hate formality, in any case. I don't think Charlie will mind, and I hope that you will not."

"Oh, no. I mean—of course not, Harry."

"I think you must know that I have come to care for you very much, Sophia, and hope that you will do me the honor of becoming my wife."

"Oh—no. I—I don't think—" Sophia had no idea what she was saying, her mind seemed to be a turmoil of emotions, none of them familiar enough for her to feel safe with.

"Sophia, I know that it is fashionable for ladies to refuse the first time, and that the gentleman is then expected to prove he is in earnest by trying again, or even several times. I hoped we might just dispense with all of that foolishness," he said with a smile, in an effort to calm her.

"Of course we can dispense with it, Harry. It's just that I—"

"You are surprised, but surely you must have been expecting it, my dear."

"Well, yes," she said simply, "but I was not sure that I—"

"Sophia, you must forgive me if I have been taking too much for granted," he said, trying not to let his heart leap about in this hopeful way. "If you do not care for me, believe me I will understand and not pursue the matter any further. We will remain friends, I hope."

"Oh no, Harry, it is not that at all. Of course I care for you very much." She hastened to reassure him, thinking that she had hurt him dreadfully by her equivocation, and feeling surer of herself in the role of comforter, she patted his hand and said, in an almost motherly tone, "And of course I shall be honored to be your wife."

Ignoring the leaden feeling in his chest, he took both of her hands in his and kissed them warmly. She leaned forward, thinking that he might now want to kiss her, but he only smiled upon her, and asked if she would mind attending a dinner at his mother's to meet some of his mother's friends.

"I know it might be boring, my dear, but it would give my mother pleasure. And of course I hope that your whole family will be able to come."

"Of course, Harry, we shall all be delighted to come."

"Good. Then I will settle a date with Mallory. Now I think I should go and speak to Charlie, don't you?"

"Oh, yes. Well, he will be in his library, I think."

He kissed her hands again, bowed, and left her. She sat staring after him for a moment in astonishment. Never had she imagined a proposal to be like this. So calm, she thought unreasonably, so—so—dispassionate! *Why, he might have been asking me to go riding in the morning!* She felt slightly indignant and slightly deflated.

Finally she went to find Mallory, feeling the need to be comforted and made much of.

When Augusta returned from her trip to the silk warehouse, she found the house quiet, and except for Charlie, deserted. The butler, taking her bundles from her, informed her that the master was in his library, so she went directly there.

She found him lounging in front of his fire with a book.

"Charlie, where has everyone gone?" she asked throwing aside her bonnet.

"Oh, I think Mallory had some shopping to do and took Soph with her."

"But Soph said she didn't want to go shopping when I asked her to come along with me this morning."

"Oh, I think she was feeling a bit—restless. We had Carnmoor to call this morning."

"You had—oh—I see," she said, turning her face away to look into the fire.

"Yes, all the women in fits, of course. He made his proposal and then came to tell me she had accepted and he hoped I didn't mind."

"She—accepted," Augusta stated flatly.

"Yes, and I must admit that I wasn't so sure she would, though Mallory thought it was a certainty all along," Charlie responded, sliding a careful look around at her. He had not been insensitive to the tone of her voice just now. She was less pleased than he would have expected her to be. *Now, what's afoot here,* he wondered.

"Well," she said, with a somewhat shaky little laugh, "our Soph shall be a duchess. She must be walking on air."

"Actually she didn't seem to be as excited as Mallory. Perhaps she was just too overcome to express herself," he replied.

"Yes, perhaps. Charlie," she said after a pause, "do you think this will hurt Courtley?"

"Bound to. I've known he was in love with Sophia this age. Surprised she never saw it."

"I don't think he ever told her how he felt. It's too bad, in a way, for I think if he had—well, that's neither here nor there. Charlie, I think I will go up to my room for a bit of rest. I find all that shopping has tired me."

After she was gone, Charlie sat staring into the fire, trying to figure the whole thing out. Here was Sophia acting less than thrilled, and now Augusta behaving as though she were—what?—in pain? Yes, it was a careful, stilted way of speaking, as though to cover pain. Now what could this be about, he wondered. Augusta could never be so stupid as to be envious of Sophia's attaching a duke. Even less could he imagine her feeling that her few moments ahead of Sophia in the world entitled her to be the first to become engaged; that was practiced in some families where the girls were married off strictly in order of precedence. Could she possibly be already grieving in anticipation of the loss of her twin, so close to her always?

Finally, he gave it up. He must just discuss it with Mallory. Mallory could fathom these moods and emotions much better than he.

Augusta, in her room, far from appearing weary, as

she had claimed to Charles, was marching herself from window to dressing table to bedside, around and around, her chin up and her mouth in a firm line.

You will not *cry,* she told herself firmly, *you will not* dare *to cry. You were warned weeks ago that this was surely going to happen, you were told not to allow yourself to feel the way you were about Harry, and you have no one to blame but yourself if you feel the way you do now. Undoubtedly the pain will cease after awhile, and finally wear away altogether. Meanwhile, there is Sophia to think of, and she will certainly be expecting a smiling, excited face when she returns.*

Augusta had finally managed to calm herself somewhat when the maid tapped on the door to tell her that Mr. Bramforth Wixton was below and asking if Augusta could receive him. She started to say that she could not, but decided that even Bramforth would be better than being alone with her thoughts any longer.

Chapter Thirteen

Bramforth rose from the sofa and bowed as Augusta entered the drawing room.

"Ah, Miss Portman, how kind of you to receive me," he said, taking her hand and bending to kiss her fingers.

"Not at all, Mr. Wixton. Will you take some refreshments?"

"Well, a glass of madeira, perhaps, and a biscuit might not come amiss."

"Certainly. Won't you be seated." She crossed to ring for the butler, who came in immediately and took her order and withdrew. Augusta sat down facing Bramforth.

"You are looking most charming today, Miss Portman. Such a lovely day. My—er—my mother spoke of seeing you this morning in the park."

"Oh, yes," she answered indifferently.

"Yes. She mentioned that she was a little surprised to see you holding hands with some gentleman."

"Holding hands? I cannot think what she could mean by that, Mr. Wixton," said Augusta, genuinely puzzled.

"Some gentleman you were riding with, she said."

"Oh, Mr. Madderson, but we were not—" then she remembered that they had shaken hands very briefly at one point. But why should Mrs. Wixton think—and then Augusta felt a flush of anger. *Stupid, gossiping old woman! How dare she spy on me and then go about spreading stories?*

"Your mother was mistaken in what she saw, Mr. Wixton," she said coldly.

"Oh, she meant no harm, Miss Portman. Just mentioned it to me as a trifling thing, though perhaps a bit indiscreet."

"If it is indiscreet to shake a gentleman's hand, this is the first I've heard of it!"

"Well, she cares very much for your reputation, Miss Portman, so she—"

"I think my credit is good enough that I won't need to worry your mother about my reputation, Mr. Wixton."

"Oh, it's no *worry* to her, Miss Portman. Well, I mean to say she is happy to—"

"Happy to be worried about my reputation?" inquired Augusta icily.

"No—well, yes—the fact is, you see, she thinks of you in a very particular way. A motherly way, if you understand me."

"I'm afraid that I do *not* understand you, sir. However, though I'm sure it is very kind of your mother, you may tell her that it will not be necessary for her so to concern herself."

Williams entered at this point with a tray, and served Bramforth with a glass of wine and a plate of biscuits. Bramforth, much relieved for a breathing space, absently ate his way through the entire plate without speaking. He was finding this love-making business very heavy going. Obviously, since she had come down to receive him quite alone, she was more than willing to see him. This reserve she was exhibiting was probably only maidenly shyness. Bruce Coverly had counseled him to treat her with some

112

roughness, but he really didn't feel quite up to that kind of exertion today. He had had to walk all the way over here, after all, and he was more than a little tired. However, enough of this procrastination. He set aside his wine glass and dusted the crumbs from his fingertips, then rising, he came to sit gingerly on the edge of the sofa beside Augusta.

"Miss Portman," he said possessing himself of her hand, "will you allow me to call you Augusta?"

"I would prefer that you did not, Mr. Wixton," she replied, pulling away her hand.

"Of course, of course, I understand that you are shy, dear Miss Portman. All in good time, all in good time. We will become better acquainted first, eh? I have hopes that we will be very good friends, indeed, before much longer, my dear."

"Mr. Wixton, I am somewhat wearied from a long shopping trip. I'm going to ask you to excuse me now."

"Miss Portman, please." He slipped to one knee with a thud. "You must allow me to speak."

"I would prefer that you did not, Mr. Wixton," she said, attempting to rise.

He took her hand and literally pulled her back down onto the couch. "You must allow me, Miss Portman. My heart is much too full to endure silence for another moment."

"Mr. Wixton, you will oblige me by stopping this at once. I cannot believe that you are so insensitive you will persist when I tell you that it is distasteful to me," said Augusta firmly.

"I understand, my dear Miss Portman."

"I am not your dear Miss Portman!"

"No, no, of course not. Forgive my impetuosity if you will be so kind, and understand that my love for you makes me forget myself."

"Mr. Wixton, I do not know what maggot you have got in your brain about me. I cannot believe you feel anything like love for me. Why, you hardly know me."

"All in good time, my de—Miss Portman, all in good time. When one is struck by love at first encounter, as I have been, there is little time for encompassing the finer details. One simply gallops ahead, full of passion and ardor, wanting only to—"

Augusta's sense of humor finally overcame her indignation at the picture of this lumbering, obese man, with his air of being half-asleep most of the time, galloping about in a passion of love. She began to giggle, and then went into paroxysms of laughter that caused the tears to stream down her face.

Bramforth, halted in mid-sentence, watched her in amazement for a moment, and then began to beam.

"Very good, Miss Portman, very good. I have made you merry, you see. Oh we shall go along famously, always being jolly together."

Augusta wiped her eyes and tried by taking deep breaths to calm herself.

"I am sorry, Mr. Wixton. Something just struck me as very funny."

"Oh, I quite understand, I quite understand. Think of it no more, I quite enjoy to see you so happy. I hope that I can always make you so."

Augusta, realizing he was preparing to start all over, made to rise again, but he immediately seized her hand and, clinging to it firmly, forced her to remain seated, unless she was willing to go through an undignified struggle.

"Miss Portman. I came today to ask you to be my wife. You know that I love you and I have every reason to believe you are not indifferent to me."

"Thank you, Mr. Wixton. I would have preferred that you not speak, but since you have done so, I will give you a very straight and conclusive answer. *No*. No, now, and no, very definitely. I do not love you, I could never love you, and I wish you will not ever bring up the subject again in the future." And with that, Augusta rose quickly before he could stop her again and went to the door and held it open for him.

Bramforth with the aid of the sofa, hauled himself to his feet with some difficulty, and crossed to the door.

"Dear lady, I understand completely. You are all proper

114

maidenly shyness and I have taken you by surprise. I honor those sweet feelings and will give you time to get used to the idea and then come to you again."

"Good day, Mr. Wixton," said Augusta, realizing the futility of protest. He bowed, and strutted grandly out. She closed the door firmly behind him. *Well,* she thought, it was most unpleasant, *but it certainly took my mind off other things for awhile.*

By the time Sophia and Mallory returned from their shopping trip, Augusta had had plenty of time to compose herself, and was able to face Sophia with a smiling face.

Sophia came into their bedroom, where Augusta was preparing to change for dinner, and Augusta flew to her to embrace her with many kisses and exclamations, to congratulate her.

"Sophia, my dearest sister, I am *so* happy for you. I have been seething with impatience all afternoon to tell you," she cried, forcing enthusiasm into her voice.

"Thank you, Gussie, I felt the same. I was desolate that you were gone and I couldn't come straight to you to share it. Are you truly happy for me? You think it is a good thing?"

"Well, of course, you goose! Do you not think so yourself?"

"Yes-s-s. I suppose I am not yet used to it. I feel so stupid, Augusta, not at all the way I had thought I would feel."

"Darling, I am sure it must be a rather overwhelming experience for any young girl to fall in love and accept a proposal. You will realize the whole thing and be comfortable with it any moment now," Augusta said in a rallying tone.

"Have you been in love, Augusta?" Sophia asked somewhat hesitantly.

Augusta was so startled she could think of nothing to say for a moment. She had never lied to her twin, and did not want to do so now, and yet if she confessed that she was in love, Sophia would expect to be told who it was. There was no way she could answer without dissembling somewhat, she finally decided.

"Well, I think I am beginning to be, but it is too early to be sure."

"Oh, Gussie, how wonderful. Who is it?" Sophia asked, as Augusta had known she would.

"Mr. Madderson, but I am truly not sure of it. It is just that I enjoy his company more than most and find him warm and kind and amusing."

"Oh, I understand, Gussie. Just as I feel for Harry. I find it so confusing, actually. I had thought to feel all sort of swooning with happiness—but—well, the truth is I feel more like crying than anything else. Not very happy at all."

"Sophia, darling! Oh, do not say so. Maybe it is just the excitement that makes you feel so."

"Perhaps you are right. But—but—oh, Gussie!" And with a wail Sophia threw herself into Augusta's arms and began to cry. Augusta soothed her and told her to cry as much as she would, and such things as we say when someone cries.

"He—he—did not even—even—ki-ki-ss me!" Sophia sobbed.

"Did not *kiss* you? When he proposed, do you mean?" Sophia nodded, and cried harder, while Augusta held her and tried to think what it could mean.

"Nor has he ever kissed me," Sophia continued, "and he did not say that he loved me."

"Now, darling, perhaps you were too excited to remember it exactly. I cannot think that Harry would propose without telling you of his feelings."

"He said—said—that he ca-a-ared for me very much."

"Well, there! That is the same thing. Now you see, you are being silly."

"But he did not *kiss* me!" Sophia wailed, and began a fresh paroxysm of tears.

Augusta hugged her fiercely and thought that if Harry had been available at that moment, she would have cheerfully boxed his ears for causing her sister so much unhappiness. What could he mean by such behavior? If he loved

116

Sophia enough to propose marriage, how could he not sweep her into his arms and make love to her? After all, this was not an arranged marriage, or one of convenience. Did he think Sophia such a sensitive creature that she would be frightened if he became too impetuous? Perhaps that was the way of it, but dear Heaven, how could he be so idiotish?

"Soph, listen to me, darling. Come now, take my handkerchief and dry your eyes. Now, I think it may be that Harry senses your—your delicate nature, and was afraid of frightening you in some way if he behaved in too loverlike a way with you. He probably feels that he must go very slowly with you, and build your trust in him. Do you see?"

"But he was not loverlike in any way, Augusta. More brotherly than anything else."

"Did you tell him that you—returned his regard?"

"Yes. Well, he asked me and I said that I cared for him very much."

"Do you *love* him, Sophia?"

"I—I—thought I must. I am always so agitated when I am with him, and no one else makes me feel that way."

"Are you happy when you are with him?"

"Not always. I am uncomfortable a great deal of the time, but I thought maybe that was part of being in love."

Augusta looked at her in dismay, wondering if it was possible that Sophia did not love Harry at all, but only thought she should do so because everyone told her she ought. On the other hand there was that heartbroken cry, "he did not kiss me," which probably expressed that she loved him very much indeed, and wanted him to be more romantic.

"Darling Soph, I think all these tears are just because you are overwrought with excitement. And I make no doubt that the next time you see Harry he will be as loverlike as any girl could wish. I think he was just showing you his deep respect and regard for you, and that he was willing to wait and not take advantage of you in any way."

"Yes, yes, I suppose you are right and I'm just being

117

foolish. Thank you, dear Gussie, for putting up with my tantrums."

They hugged each other fervently, and Gussie felt her heart swell with love for this other half of herself, this gentler half that must be protected, this sweet-natured half whom Harry loved.

This last thought produced such an ache in her own heart that she wondered if she would ever be able to ease it, and for a moment longed to put her head down on Sophia's shoulder and cry and be comforted in her turn.

Chapter Fourteen

Bramforth dutifully reported to his mother on his return from calling upon Augusta.

"My dear, how thrilling. And what did she say?" asked Mrs. Wixton eagerly.

"Said no, of course."

Her face fell. "Said 'no'? But—but—"

"Don't disturb yourself, Mama. She behaved just as I would expect her to. I know something of these things, and I could see she was overcome by shyness, and that I am expected to persist."

"Overcome by shyness? Miss Portman?" queried Mrs. Wixton doubtfully.

"Oh, I make no doubt it was just a pretense. Young ladies are taught to behave in that way," he said with great confidence.

"Yes, that is true, of course. It's just that I would never have expected Miss Portman to be missish at all. But you feel encouraged to think—"

"Oh yes. She received me alone, and offered me refreshments, and then we laughed together and had a most jolly time. I feel sure she has been expecting my proposal any time this past week. I've not been behindhand in showing her my feelings, you know."

"I'm sure you have not, Bramsforth. But if I were you, I would not wait too long before presenting myself again. You know how young girls are. They expect you to behave with resolution. You must be quite masterful with her, sweep her off her feet, as it were. Do you understand me?"

"Sweep her off her feet?" he repeated, with an expression of distaste for what seemed to him a project promising a great deal of exertion.

"Yes, exactly, that's what young girls like above all else. We are all romantic and respond to a swaggering, arrogant sort of man who gives us no chance to dither about."

"I think I will consult my friend, Bruce Coverly. He's had much experience in these matters."

"A good idea, Bramforth," she said admiringly. "No doubt he will tell you the same thing and just how to set about it."

Mrs. Wixton decided that it would be a good thing to call upon Mrs. Portman and find out if there was any reaction in the family to Bramforth's proposal, and if possible put in a good word or two. It could not hurt, she felt sure, and it might do Bram a great deal of good, if his mother showed that she was very much in favor of the match. After all, the approval of the mother-in-law meant a lot to young girls.

The next morning, therefore, she presented herself at the Portman front door, and Mallory had no recourse but to receive her. She was entertaining young Beaumont when Mrs. Wixton was announced, and his face when he heard the dread name was a study in horrified dismay. He hastily folded up the poem he had composed the evening before and was preparing to dedicate to his goddess, and bid Mallory a hurried farewell. Mallory began to laugh as he exited, swerving in a wide path around Mrs. Wixton as she entered, as though afraid that she might in some way detain him.

"What a strange young man," commented Mrs. Wixton, staring after him. "Seems to have no manners at all."

"How do you do, Mrs. Wixton. Won't you sit down?" said Mallory, trying to swallow her laughter.

"Thank you, Mrs. Portman. My, my, you are looking in extraordinarily good health today, I must say."

"Yes, I believe I *am* in very good health these days," Mallory replied good-naturedly.

"And how are the two young ladies?"

"Sophia and Augusta? Why, they are well."

"My Bramforth came to visit Miss Portman yesterday," said Mrs. Wixton archly.

"Yes? Well, how nice," said Mallory, wondering why the woman was behaving so strangely.

"Things are progressing very nicely there, I believe," stated Mrs. Wixton, her words conveying a wealth of unspoken comment.

"They are? What—er—things do you mean, Mrs. Wixton?"

"Why, Mrs. Portman, you cannot be unaware that Bramforth is trying to fix his interests with Miss Portman."

"Fix his int—oh, oh, I *see*. And you feel that things are progressing there?" asked Mallory innocently, her eyes beginning to dance with suppressed laughter.

"Oh, definitely. So well that I thought it was time the dreaded mother-in-law-to-be should show that she is not an ogress in any way. I know young girls are often terrified in these situations that the young man's parents might not be approving. But in this case, I am happy to assure you that I entirely approve of Bram's choice in a wife."

"Too kind," said Mallory faintly, so overcome by the woman's outrageous arrogance that she could think of nothing more to the point to say in reply.

"Of course, I do feel that Miss Portman is a shade volatile, but as I told the dear duchess, I feel sure marriage will calm her down."

121

"And what did the dear duchess reply?" asked Mallory, a trace of coldness beginning to appear in her voice.

"Oh she agreed with me entirely, Mrs. Portman. Such a sweet creature she is, and always such a good friend. We are both delighted at the way things are turning out, for now we shall be closer than ever, practically related!" she concluded with a gay laugh.

Mallory by now was almost beyond speech. She wondered what she could possibly say to depress this woman's pretensions. That she should actually think that because her dreadful son had condescended to bestow his favor on a Portman they were as good as married. Mallory thought, *does she really think we could be so careless of Augusta's welfare as to allow her to throw herself away on a penniless, slothful creature like Bramforth, even if Augusta had any interest in doing so?*

"Mrs. Wixton," she said slowly, trying not to betray her feelings, "I think you may be jumping ahead just a bit too quickly. Of course I'm sure it is very flattering for Augusta to know that she has roused such emotions in Bramforth, and one can only honor the seriousness of his intentions. However, I feel quite sure that Augusta's affections are not engaged in any way."

"Ah, Mrs. Portman, you must allow me to be more experienced in these things. You are hardly more than a child yourself. Bramforth assures me that Augusta has received his attentions with interest, and he is quite sure she reciprocates his feelings. Of course, she quite properly said no to his first proposal, as any well-brought-up young lady should, but I think we may all rest easy that things will come about as we want them to soon."

"I would be less than honest with you, Mrs. Wixton, if I did not tell you that as far as I am concerned, I have no wish for things to come about at all."

"Why—why—" Mrs. Wixton now seemed almost speechless herself.

"They will not suit, Mrs. Wixton," continued Mallory firmly. "And I know I speak for Augusta's brother and guardian, when I tell you that he will never allow it."

Mrs. Wixton stared at her in astonishment for a moment while she mulled over this statement. Then slowly a smile spread over her face.

"Not to worry, Mrs. Portman. I am sure we can make him change his mind. He would not stand in the way of young love, I feel sure. When he understands that Bramforth and Augusta are serious, I'm sure he will not stand in the way of her happiness."

Mallory decided she had had more than enough for one morning, and that there was nothing more that she could profitably say to this woman.

"Mrs. Wixton, I fear I must be very rude. I have another appointment and must go and make ready or I shall be late."

"Oh, quite all right, my dear. As a matter of fact, if you are going out, perhaps you will be so kind as to take me up in your carriage as far as my house. It is not far, of course, but can be most tiresome for an old lady when she must walk."

Mallory was now forced to go out, though she had in truth no appointment. But she resigned herself to the inevitable, and nodded with good grace. She decided the Portmans must watch what they were about, for this woman was so determined, so implacable, so impervious to insult that she might catch them all off guard and have her own way in spite of all they could do.

The following day, Bram, catching sight of Bruce Coverly at their club, hailed him.

"Just the fellow I want to talk to, Coverly. Have something I want to consult you about."

"Well, speak more quietly, Wixton. My head is in a very bad way this morning. Should have been with us last night. Went to Coxton's, and there were some little birds there who know how to make a man enjoy himself, I can tell you. Oh, we had a roaring time, all drunk as lords. But today I am paying for it."

"Sorry, and all that. But here's the thing. I've said my piece to Miss Portman, and she's given me the first refusal. Only to be expected, I understand. The thing is my mother advises that I sweep her off her feet. 'Fraid someone else will get there before me. I tried to pooh-pooh the notion, for I think I'm a good judge of these things, and I tell you the lady is not unwilling, just playing coy, don't you see? Still I thought it would be a good thing to consult you. You're the expert in love matters, eh? Eh?" Bramforth brayed with laughter and poked his friend suggestively in the ribs.

"Here! None of that. I told you I'm in a bad way today," Bruce snarled.

"Oh, sorry, old fellow. But what do you say? What will be my next move?"

Bruce studied him for a few moments in silence, wondering how he could advise Bram in a way to cause the most unhappiness to the Portmans. Bruce was an extremely small-minded man, not one to give up a grudge easily, and he felt he had many scores to settle with the Portmans. To begin with there was the matter of his sister, Letitia. In spite of knowing the truth of the matter, that Letitia had thrown Charles Portman over when she had met Lord Hastings, Bruce still felt that Charles should not have accepted so eagerly, especially after Bruce had found out the true state of affairs with Hastings, and after Bruce had had his first encounter with Letitia's husband, Lord Balfount. That gentleman, in spite of having more money that he knew what to do with, had let Bruce know in no uncertain terms, that there was absolutely no point in applying to him for a bit of the ready. Tight old screw he was, and a stony-hearted old skinflint when it came to letting go of a few pounds. Bruce, in his mind, had come to blame Charles for this deplorable state of affairs.

Then there was the night of the Portman ball when he had been so shabbily treated by everyone. Rebuffed by that silly girl, when all he had wanted was a kiss, and then slapped around and thrown out of the house. He wouldn't mind getting a bit of his own back against that family.

"Well, well, what do you say," said Bramforth, "what's the best way to set about this thing? Shall I just wait a few days, or even a week, and then ask again, or follow my mother's advice. and press my cause in some other way."

"Give me a moment, Wixton, let me think. Sweep her off her feet, eh," he mused. Then he sniggered. "Elope with her!"

"Elope! Oh, I don't think—I mean to say, not done, old fellow. Family wouldn't like it, and all that," protested Bramforth.

"But they'd be faced with a *fait accompli,* don't you see, and would have to put a good face on it before the world. Impetuous youth and all that." And Bruce began to laugh, thinking of the consternation of those high-in-the-instep Portmans faced with the disgrace of an elopement.

"Well, I shouldn't know how to carry off such a thing. Besides, not my style, you know," said Bram, automatically against anything that promised to involve him in a great deal of unnecessary action.

"Nonsense, nothing to it really. Just whisk her into a carriage and drive away with her."

"But—but—she might not like such high-handed behavior."

"Don't be such a wet goose, Wixton. Course she will like it. All girls like that romantical sort of stuff."

"You really think so, eh? Well, I suppose you know better than I. But still—here, the thing's impossible. I have no carriage!"

"I'll lend you mine."

"Now, really, Coverly, I can hardly run away to the Border in an open carriage."

"All right, all right. You could hire one, I suppose."

"Can't do that, old man. Pockets to let."

"Well then, I'll get the loan of one. I know a fellow who would let me have his for a few days. Owes me."

"And his horses? And what about changes on the way? Can't drive one pair of horses all the way to the Border," said Bram, almost hopefully, still feeling that this was a great deal of trouble to be going to.

"I'll lend you the money! For God's sakes, Wixton, have some backbone, do. Here you come to me and ask me what you should do, and I spend all this time advising you in spite of the way I feel. I've offered you the carriage, I've told you I'd lend you money. What more do you want?"

"I'm just not so sure this is the way I should be going on. Not my style, you know."

"But that's just the thing. You've been hanging out for an heiress this past five years, and here's one as good as in your grasp, and you haven't got enough enterprise to take her when everything is being made easy for you. I wash my hands of you!"

And with that he turned and pretended to walk away, but not before Bram, as he knew he would, caught his arm.

"Here, don't fly up into the boughs. I didn't say I wouldn't do it. I was just trying to see all sides of the problem."

"Well, I don't like to be made to waste my time, you know," said Bruce huffily.

"No such thing. I think you're absolutely right. I must bow to your better judgment. After all, my mother said the same thing, in a way. And besides, if one consults an expert, one must be prepared to take his advice. I'll do it! Yes, by gad, I'll do it. Take her by surprise, eh?"

"That's the way," said Bruce, giving him a clap on the back. "Knew you were just that sort of fellow."

"But look here, how'll I get her into the carriage?"

"Good God, Wixton, must I tell you everything? Ask her to go for a drive with you. Nothing simpler."

"Right. I'll ask her and then I'll come and you'll get the same thing, in a way. And besides, if one consults an Diltons' party."

And ask her he did, that very evening. Only to be told that she was already promised for the next day. With the blind imperviousness of his mother, Bram inquired of her plans for the next day, and one after that. When they had been through almost a week of days, Augusta told him that she felt it would be better if they did not see each other alone any more, since he would not take her "no" as final.

126

Bramforth, already convinced that Augusta regarded him with favor, put this down to girlish playfulness, and simply smiled forgivingly at her. His mind was really busy with the problem of how to get her into his carriage when her schedule was so full. Could he get the carriage for a few extra days, he wondered, and then sort of hang about to find her coming from a shop one day? No, that would be difficult, since she would be bound to have someone with her, if only her maid or a footman. Nice young ladies never went unattended on the streets.

He finally decided he must consult Bruce Coverly on so thorny a problem.

Chapter Fifteen

"*The Duchess of Carnmoor. Please ask Mrs. Portman if she is receiving,*" demanded the duchess in ringing tones, and a cowed Williams almost stumbled in his haste to show her into the drawing room. He flung open the drawing-room door, announced her in obviously impressed tone, and bowed as she marched grandly past him.

Mallory rose and came to lead her to the sofa. "Your Grace, how very nice of you to call. Will you have some refreshments?"

"No, thank you, my dear, never take anything this early in the day. Ruinous to my digestion, I find. You are certainly looking blooming. In the family way?" she asked bluntly.

Mallory blushed, but smiled and acknowledged that it was so.

"Good. Should have 'em while you're young. Waited too long with Harry, gave me a difficult time. However, he was worth waiting for."

"He was indeed. A wonderful boy, dear Harry. We are all very fond of him."

"Well, since he and Sophia have made up their minds, that's a very good thing, isn't it? Must say, I am quite delighted myself. Not that I ever had any doubts that Harry had good taste and would not disgrace me when it came to choosing a wife."

"How kind of you, Your Grace. I'm sure Sophia is very fortunate."

"Couldn't agree with you more. Chose just such a man as Harry myself, and never regretted it a day in my life."

She gave Mallory a glowing description of her deceased husband, and as she talked her sharp, abrupt way of speaking softened, as did her face, and Mallory began to respond with great warmth to this charming old lady and realize that her imperiousness was all part of the role she imagined herself in.

"Ah well, I mustn't bore you any longer with these old stories. We have a new one unfolding, which is much more important today. That's why I've come. I would like to give a small dinner party for some of my old friends to introduce Sophia to them. Will next week suit you, Mrs. Portman? Harry will have put the announcements in the *Times* by then, so everyone will have heard of it and be most eager to meet her."

"Next week will be fine. Any day you say," agreed Mallory.

"Very well then, I'll say Wednesday. I hope you will not be bored by all of my old cronies, you are such a young family, but it will only be for a few hours."

"Nonsense, dear duchess. I'm sure your friends could not be boring. We shall all be delighted to meet them."

Lord Beaumont and Lord Hastings were announced at this point, and after greeting Mallory, bent solicitously over the duchess' hand.

She inquired graciously about their families, and then settled back against the sofa, obviously delighted to find herself in the company of two such handsome young men. She watched with twinkling amusement as Lord Beaumont took out a sheet of paper from his pocket and unfolded it, only to refold it and regretfully return it to his pocket. She was well acquainted with the fashionable new custom for young married women to have young unattached men hanging about, professing to be in love with them, and writing poems in praise of their beauty. She quite envied Mrs. Portman in having two such attractive men paying court to her. *In my day I should have had just as many myself,* she thought with great satisfaction, and just a touch of wistfulness.

Lord Hastings came to sit beside the duchess and began to flirt with her outrageously, much to her gratification.

"My dear duchess, it is not in the least fair in you to refuse to grow old. You quite put the rest of us to shame. Your complexion must be the despair of every young girl who sees you."

"No reason why it should be. I'll be happy to tell her how to have just such rosy cheeks as mine," she said, with a delighted laugh.

"What do you recommend? Diet, exercise, ten hours' sleep every night?"

"Rouge!" she exclaimed, and cackled happily.

"You are trying to gammon me, Your Grace, and well you know it. Such color could not come from a pot. Now, will you promise to save the first waltz for me at the next ball?"

"You are just such a wicked rascal as your father, Hastings. Oh, the stories I could tell you of that gentleman. You may favor your mother in looks, but I think in every other way you must take after him."

Augusta and Sophie made an entrance into this happy conversation, and the duchess pulled Sophia down onto the sofa next to her and hugged her soundly. Sophia, all shy blushes and smiles kissed her cheek, and then the duchess demanded that Augusta come and kiss her also, now they were practically related. This declaration made it necessary to reveal to Hastings and Beaumont the news of Sophia's and Harry's engagement, and the room for some moments resounded with felicitations.

"Well, Mrs. Portman, I must congratulate you on having such an interesting *salon*. I don't know when I've enjoyed myself so much," boomed the duchess.

"I hope you will condescend to become part of it more often, Your Grace," responded Mallory. She gently pulled her hand away from Beaumont, who had clasped it fervently in an effort to get her entire attention, and she rose to come and join the duchess on the sofa. Hastings made way for her with many protestations of regret and went to join Augusta.

"Miss Portman, I hope we will soon be offering *you* our congratulations," he said teasingly.

"Very kind of you, Lord Hastings," she replied with a smile, "but I fear that will be some time in coming."

"Not if I'm any judge. I have noticed that Mr. Madderson has been most assiduous in his attentions," he said, studying her quizzically.

"I declare, Lord Hastings, you are as bad as any society gossip I've met in London. I must beg you not to start any such hares as that," she protested with a laugh.

"My lips are sealed, my dear Miss Portman. But in return I shall expect to be told at once if anything interesting does come about. I count Hampton one of my friends and would be very happy if his suit were to be successful. He's a fine fellow," he said with great sincerity.

"He is indeed. You have made a great hit with the duchess," she responded, deliberately changing the subject.

"I have ever been more successful with old ladies than with young, alas," he said, his eyes twinkling.

"I think it is more likely that you do not practice much with young ones because you are afraid of being trapped," she said shrewdly.

"I am discovered! You are much too sharp for me, Miss Portman."

Charles now entered the drawing room, with Hampton Madderson behind him. They both stopped abruptly, and Charles stared in amazement at the large company assembled before him.

"Charles, I'm so glad you came. Here is the Duchess of Carnmoor come to call," cried Mallory.

Charles came to welcome the duchess to his home and to introduce Hampton Madderson to her. The duchess looked up with only a hint of coquetry.

"Pleasure, Mr. Madderson. Well, Mr. Portman, I must say I can't remember being in a drawing room in London that contained so many handsome young men. I believe the Portman women have captured them all."

"They have certainly captured the best of all with Harry, Your Grace," responded Charles.

"Yes," she said, nodding with satisfaction. "Harry is a wonderful son for any mother to claim, and I do so proudly. And I'm just as proud of his choice in a bride, Mr. Portman. Dear little Sophia." Here she patted Sophia's cheek. "Such a delightful child."

Hampton had, during this exchange of compliments, made his way to Augusta's side, and Hastings went to join Mallory and the duchess.

"Miss Portman, I hear I am to congratulate your family upon your sister's engagement," he said taking her hand to kiss her fingers lightly.

"Yes, thank you, Mr. Madderson. And how do you do today?"

"Better now that I am with you. When I am not, I always fear you are something I dreamed."

"A nightmare, perhaps," she inquired with a studied seriousness.

"My conscience is too clear for me to ever have nightmares, Miss Portman, though I must admit the *quality* of my dreams has improved since I've met you."

"How very gratifying, to be sure. My head shall be quite turned if you continue, Mr. Madderson."

"Now you are teasing me, for well I know that you are used to much more extravagant compliments than that. However, I thrive on competition. Puts me on my mettle, makes me try harder. Ah, now you are laughing at me, Miss Portman, but I assure you I am entirely serious." He lowered his voice slightly and leaned toward her, "The game is over for me, you see, and now I am playing for keeps."

Her eyes flew up to his face, at the seriousness of his tone, and for a moment they stared wordlessly at each other. Then Augusta looked away in confusion from the love she saw in his eyes, at the same time wishing desperately that it was possible for her to return it, for she liked him so well.

Mallory had watched this encounter, and felt her heart swell with happiness to think that it now seemed possible that both of her dear girls were to be so happily settled. She turned back to find the duchess turning from the scene at the same time, and their eyes met in happy complicity.

"Very nice, indeed. I know that young man's mother, or did many years ago. We neither of us go about much any longer so we've lost touch. But they are a fine family, and certainly well enough off to be a most eligible *parti* for any young lady," said the duchess.

"He seems a delightful young man, though we have not known him for very long," said Mallory. "However, it begins to seem that we may know him very much better before long."

Bramforth, meanwhile, had spent the morning trying to find his friend, Bruce Coverly. After checking the usual places with no luck, he finally found him walking along the street in front of White's.

"Coverly, thank goodness, I've looked everywhere for you. Need another consultation."

"Net the little bird, did you? When will you need the carriage?"

"That's just it, you see. Couldn't get her to come. I don't think I've ever encountered a girl with such a full social calendar. It will be weeks, it seems, before she could be free. Also said she thought we should not meet alone anymore, but that's all a hum, don't you think? Part of the act?"

"Oho, did she now? Well, we must think about this," said Bruce. Now, of course, Bruce Coverly was as well aware as the Duchess of Carnmoor of the unsuitability of Bram as an eligible husband for a girl such as Augusta Portman. However, not for a moment would he reveal his awareness, for he didn't want in any way to discourage Bram. Bruce had grown more enthusiastic about his elopement scheme the more he thought of it, and chuckled in spiteful glee every time he pictured the Portmans' consternation.

His slippery mind went to work at once on this new problem, and before long he had come up with a plan he felt sure would work.

"We must first decide on the day," he said.

"The day? What day?" asked Bramforth.

"The day for your elopement, you cabbagehead! What else are we talking of?"

"Well. No use rushing things. Some day next week should do."

"Next week! Well, I must say, there's not much of the eager lover about you, Bram. I should have expected you to say tomorrow."

"No, next week," said Bramforth firmly, with the unexpected stubbornness of the stupid.

"Oh, all right. Your elopement, I suppose. Now, what day next week?"

"Any day you say," replied Bramforth. Having won his point he was now willing to be generous.

"Wednesday, then. We'll say Wednesday. Now the thing to do is take the carriage to someplace near the Portman house and then go on foot to watch for Mrs. Portman to leave the house."

"*Mrs.* Portman? No, no, Coverly, you've got the wrong way of it. It's *Miss* Portman I—"

"Will you please be quiet and listen? I shan't go on if you keep interrupting!"

"Very well, no need to get in a huff. Just thought you had the wrong—"

"Bramforth!" said Coverly warningly.

"Sorry, sorry, go ahead." Bram placated him.

"Right. Now, when you see Mrs. Portman leave the house you wait for a bit and then get the carriage and drive to the door in a tearing hurry, and rush up and explain that Mrs. Portman has had an accident in her carriage and Miss Portman must come to her immediately. She'll come all right. Then, Bob's your uncle."

"But what if Mrs. Portman doesn't go out of the house all day?" objected Bramforth.

"Hmmm. Yes, there is that possibility, though I thought women always went out at some time during the day. Well, let me think now. How if we wrote a note from the duchess asking if Mrs. Portman would mind dropping by for a chat about wedding plans or something. Mrs. Portman will undoubtedly go rushing right around."

"But when she gets there the duchess will tell her she didn't write the note, and then what will happen?"

"Why should we concern ourselves with that? By that time you'll have the girl in the carriage with you and be well away."

"True," said Bram admiringly. "I say, you are as smart as you can stare, Coverly."

They continued to discuss the scheme, trying to polish off all the rough edges and plan ahead for any contingencies. When Bramforth said what should he do if Miss Sophia came to the door instead of Miss Portman, Coverly said he could be perfectly assured that if Mrs. Portman was summoned by the duchess to discuss wedding plans she would take Miss Sophia with her. But it didn't matter. Bram would be very careful to ask for Miss Portman and rush her away before anyone else could make an appearance.

They parted with mutual congratulations upon what clever fellows they were.

Chapter Sixteen

After dinner that night, Charles finally found an opportu-
nity to speak privately with his wife. The twins had gone
out to a ball in the company of Harry, and the Portmans
were comfortably settled before their drawing-room fire.

Charles was sleepily watching Mallory embroidering im-
possibly tiny flowers on to something that he felt sure must
be a baby dress.

"My darling, I fear you will ruin your eyes doing that
in this light. Should you not wait for daylight to do such
fine work?"

She laughed softly, "You know you are not worried
about my eyes, Charles. You just want my attention. Is
something worrying you?"

"Well, yes, now that you mention it," he answered,
sitting up straighter, "it's Augusta, actually."

"Augusta? What about her?"

"I can't quite put my finger on it, Mal. But something
is not right with her, you may depend upon it."

"Was it a specific incident that worries you, or just a general air?"

"Well, take the day when I told her of Soph's engagement. She'd been out when all the excitement happened, and then when she came back you and Soph were out, so I told her. I'll vow she was not happy at the news. Do you think she is sort of anticipating losing Soph? They've always been so close."

"No," responded Mallory firmly. "I don't thing it could be that. Augusta is much too sensible for that to affect her so much you would notice it."

"Then what can it be?"

"I don't know, my dear," said Mallory thoughtfully. "I must speak to her myself and see if I see it. I feel terrible to think that I have been so engrossed in my own feelings—the baby and Sophia's engagement—that I haven't seen this for myself."

"Now, now, don't start berating yourself or I shall be sorry I spoke at all. You know I don't like you to fret over them."

"But I have been negligent. Well, never mind, I won't keep on about it, but I shall speak to her at the first opportunity."

But several days were to pass before such an opportunity presented itself. At breakfast the next morning it was decided that there must be new dresses for the girls to wear to the duchess' dinner party, which made a call to the silk warehouses an urgent necessity. This was followed by frenzied consultations with the dressmaker.

Sophia's gown was to be white gauze opening over white satin, the tiny puffed sleeves to be embroidered with rosettes of silver sequins. Augusta chose pale orange crepe over white satin, trimmed with Brussels lace. Mallory had declared she would wear her pink silk, which had only made one appearance so far this season; besides the dressmaker would have quite enough to do getting the girls' dresses ready in time.

This activity, combined with frequent callers, and social obligations made a private talk impossible before Saturday. Mallory by this time had begun to notice certain signs of strain in Augusta, and immediately after breakfast demanded Augusta's company for a drive in a tone of voice that brooked no refusal.

They rode along for some time in silence, while Mallory in her mind tried and rejected several openings. Augusta, a slightly bewildered expression on her face, eyed the resolute profile beside her. She knew that look well enough to know that Mallory had some bee in her bonnet.

"Mallory, dear," said Augusta, finally unable to bear the suspense any longer. "Is anything wrong?"

"Wrong? Of course not, darling. In fact, everything is wonderful, much more wonderful than I have yet told you. I had meant to wait with my secret until we were all together, but everyone is so busy these days," she said somewhat plaintively.

"Mallory! Please, get to the secret!"

"Well—" Mallory blushed rosily. "I am—that is—we are—I am to have a child," she finished all in a rush.

Augusta emitted a most unladylike squeal, causing several startled pedestrians to stare, and threw herself upon Mallory with exclamations of delight. They hugged and kissed and cried a bit, and finally sat back, clasping hands, and beamed into each other's flushed and happy faces.

"I'm to be an *aunt*," sighed Augusta ecstatically. "It is of all things what I would like most!"

"Can you imagine the bewilderment of the poor little thing, trying to puzzle out which aunt is which?" Mallory began to giggle.

"We shall probably blend into but one aunt for a long time, unless we take to wearing always the same color. You know, primrose for Soph and green for me, or something like that."

"And no doubt Sophia will soon follow my example and then we shall have yours one day. Oh, I love the thought of so many babies!" Mallory sighed blissfully, and slid a look at Augusta.

"Yes, lovely." Augusta changed the subject. "When did you say we may expect this new relative?"

"Around Christmas, I think, is a safe guess."

"Oh, wonderful! We shall all be at Linbury. No baby could possibly want to be born anyplace nicer."

"My own feelings exactly. I only hope Sophia and Harry will decide to wait until after the new year for their wedding. I think spring will be nice, don't you?"

"I'm sure Sophia will not dream of getting married if you were not able to be there, so don't worry about it."

"I know. I do tend to fret, Charles tells me so. I am so happy for her."

"You haven't told her about the baby yet? Good. Then I shall tell her as soon as I see her. You won't mind?"

Mallory assured her she would not mind at all. She had carefully listened to Augusta's tone throughout this exchange, and had not missed her reluctance to discuss Sophia's engagement. *No,* she thought, *not really reluctance, but a certain—elusiveness.* A sort of shying away from the subject. So Charles was right, and it did have something to do with Sophia's coming marriage.

"We must put our heads together soon and plan her dress, and yours, of course, for you will attend her," Mallory said enthusiastically, having decided that the only way to deal with this problem was by frontal attack.

"Oh, we've plenty of time for that, surely. I'm much more interested in your opinion on a bonnet I saw yesterday. Why don't we go to the shop, and you shall see for yourself if it suits me."

"Very well, my dear," said Mallory equably, leaning forward to give the directions to her coachman. She had now enough hints to make her more determined than ever to get to the bottom of this enigma, and an agreeable hour trying on bonnets would give her time to plan how to attack the problem. Should she just bide her time and be watchful, or come right out and ask Augusta what was wrong? She hated prying in this roundabout way, but at the same time she could not bear for Augusta to be unhappy and have no one to talk to.

On the return trip, therefore, she opted for straightforwardness.

"Augusta, it seems to me that you are not so happy as

I would want you to be. Can you tell me what is bothering you and let me help if I can?"

For one brief moment Augusta stared at her, her eyes wide open in surprise, and Mallory saw the brows contract the least bit, and a flash of pain was there and gone. Then—click—the shutters came down, the brow cleared, and Augusta laughed gaily.

"Really, Mallory, now you *are* imagining things, as Charles accuses you of doing."

Mallory studied her for a moment in silence, then reached out to pat her hand.

"Very well, dear one, but just remember that I am here, and Charles is here, and if ever anything is troubling you we want to know about it and try to help."

But Mallory was not fooled by that gay little laugh. She was convinced of what she had seen; something was hurting Augusta. With young girls, it was usually something involving a young man, but from what she had seen, Augusta could not be suffering from unrequited love, for Mr. Madderson exhibited every sign of being truly smitten. Augusta seemed equally interested in him, but even if she were not it surely could not be a cause of suffering for her.

Mallory decided the only thing she could do was watch very carefully and see if she could find a source for this unhappiness. And a talk with Sophia on the subject might be profitable. Even if Sophia had not noticed anything, she would be alerted and might get Augusta to confide in her.

When they arrived back at the house, it was to find Sophia holding court alone to a large gathering of morning callers, including the Boreleys', the Dilworths', Mrs. Wixton, and a rather determinedly smiling Courtley. Mallory was swept up by the ladies, but Augusta went immediately to Courtley.

"Well, Gussie, this is a happy day for Sophia, is it not?" he said, giving her shoulders a brief squeeze in his usual brotherly fashion.

"Courtley, my dear—" she began, but then had to stop as she felt her throat tighten with tears. She looked at him mutely, her face telling him that she knew this was not a happy day for *him,* but he refused to acknowledge their message.

"Yes, indeed, I know how you must feel, Gussie, but it will be your turn soon, and I feel I must take the full credit for it, since it was I who introduced you to Hampton."

Augusta swallowed the lump in her throat, and, willing the tears back, tried to smile at him. "You are being much too precipitous, Courtley. We are very good friends, Mr. Madderson and I, but there is nothing more."

"Now I *am* disappointed. He exhibits all the signs of a man truly in love, forever singing your praises, and you remain the cool Society beauty, with more suitors than you can count, rather bored by the whole thing."

"Now you malign me, Courtley, and you know it. I hope I never behave in such a way."

And so, with such surface badinage, they averted the subject closest to their hearts, and the very real need both of them felt to put their heads on a sympathetic shoulder and sob.

After luncheon, Mallory contrived to have a few moments alone with Sophia, and went straight to the point.

"Have you felt there was something bothering Augusta this past week or so, Sophia?"

Sophia looked at her with surprise. "Something bothering Gussie? Why no, I had not noticed anything. Do you feel there is something?"

"Yes, I do, and so does Charles. I am surprised that you have not noticed. But there, how should you, indeed? With all that has been happening for you these past few days, it would be wonderful if you had."

"But I should have—no, don't shake your head. She is closer to me than anyone, and if anyone should have noticed it should have been I. I'm afraid I am guilty of having been so wrapped up in my own problems that I—"

"Your problems?" Mallory interrupted her. "Why, Sophia, what problems are you speaking of?"

Sophia looked confused, "Did I say problems? I guess what I meant was 'affairs.' I have no problems, of course."

In spite of this assertion, something in her tone caused

142

Mallory to pause in her thoughts of Augusta and turn her attention to Sophia. *Now what is this?* she thought. *Can she have had a quarrel with Harry already?* Could she be having second thoughts? Or was it, perhaps, something to do with the duchess? Heavens knows, that formidable lady might give any shy young girl cause for alarm.

"Sophia, darling, is all well with you and Harry?"

"But of course it is, Mallory. Harry is everything that is required in a fiancé, and I have no quarrel with him at all," Sophia replied with a smile.

But Mallory sensed a reserve in this reply. Were these the words of a girl in love? They were certainly not the words she herself would have used with regard to darling Charles when they were first engaged.

"You do *love* Harry, Sophia?"

"Oh, indeed, darling Mal. Otherwise why would I feel this butterfly feeling in his presence? Besides, he is so sweet to me always."

Mallory found this a less than satisfactory answer, but could think of no way to express what answer she had expected. After all, love was different things to different people, and though she would have expected more romantic sighings and blushings from Sophia at this point, it might be that her basic shyness prohibited such an exhibition from her.

Mallory finally went away, feeling that her probe for an answer about Augusta had only revealed further questions. She had to admit now that in her pride at Sophia's accomplishment in attaching a duke, Mallory had not thought to inquire of Sophia whether she was truly happy at the prospect of being a duchess. She had assumed that Sophia must be very much in love with Harry to have accepted his proposal. Was it possible that Sophia had accepted for another reason? Awe of the title? A sense of obligation to her family, who seemed eager for the match? But no, surely this was not possible? Sophia would not marry where there was no love. And she had said, when asked, that she did—now what were her words? Something about her butterfly feeling. Surely an apt description of the state of being in love. *Or nerves,* said a cynical voice in Mallory's head. Good God! Was it possible that Harry made Sophia nervous, and she, poor innocent child that she was, equated that with being—

Mallory rushed downstairs to find Charlie. She felt the need suddenly to be held and soothed by the very strong masculine arms of her husband, and to have all these vague disquiets pooh-poohed away.

Chapter Seventeen

"I'll be going to Cowley's Emporium immediately after breakfast for new gloves and a spray of flowers for my pink. Would either of you care to accompany me? Or have you any commissions for me?" asked Mallory, at breakfast on the Wednesday morning of the duchess' dinner party.

"Oh, Mallory, how kind. Could you pick up some silk stockings for me? I would love to go with you, but Mrs. Needles is coming to pin up the hem of my gown an hour from now, so I dare not leave the house," said Sophia.

"Of course, darling. Now, what is this? A note from that dreadful Wixton woman. Dear heaven, the woman's effrontery knows no bounds. She knows I will not mind, she says, if she begs me, if I am going shopping this morning, to be so good as to take her up on the way. She needs just a few wee things, she says. Oh well, I suppose since I am going, I must be obliging. Augusta, say that you will accompany me. I cannot face that woman alone," said Mallory.

"I would only do this for you, Mallory, and you will remember that you are now greatly in my debt," replied Augusta sternly.

This note was the brainchild of Bramforth and Bruce, who belatedly realized that a note from the duchess, not written on her own crested notepaper, might rouse suspicions.

Bramforth, having had an unusually successful breakfast, had hit upon the idea of a note, obstensibly from his mother, that might accomplish the desired end of getting Mallory out of the house. They both felt confident that the evening being for Sophia, she would undoubtedly be in need of fripperies and would accompany Mallory. Bramforth, to insure that his mother would be dressed and waiting, told her that he had encountered Mrs. Portman who had offered to do this service for her dear friend, Mrs. Wixton. Mrs. Wixton, of course, was overcome with gratitude by this kindness, and immediately prepared a list of small articles she was in need of.

All being put in train, Bramforth was therefore loitering carefully out of sight, his carriage waiting in the next square, for the departure of Mallory.

Presently the front door of the Portman residence opened, and Mallory came down the front steps, followed by—aha! Miss Sophia, sure enough, in her primrose dress that Bramforth remembered distinctly from his first meeting with the twins.

Of course, Bramforth was not to know that though the twins never dressed alike now, they had many dresses made exactly the same, since their coloring and taste generally coincided. So it was Augusta, in primrose, following Mallory into the Portman carriage.

Bramforth proceded jauntily back to his waiting carriage and prepared to wait, as Bruce had coached him, for at least a half-hour before going for Miss Portman.

As he had planned, Bramforth made a very dashing arrival in front of the Portmans', the horses plunging and rearing as he sawed at the reins to halt them. However, he was unable to complete the next step of his picture of urgency by leaping nimbly down as a man in a great hurry would. Caution, not to mention cowardice, overcame him, and he clambered carefully and heavily down. He tried to make up for this by running up the steps and pounding authoritatively on the knocker.

Sophia, on her way through the front hall, after having lingered long at the breakfast table reading letters of congratulations from her friends at Linbury, stopped in shock at this thundering at the front door and then hurried to answer it before Williams could get there from the kitchen.

"You must come at once. Mrs. Portman—I just happened to be passing at the time—" panted Bramforth, a combination of exertion and nerves giving his tone the desired sound of emergency.

"Mallory? What has happened? Quickly, Mr. Wixton, tell me what has happened," demanded Sophia, frightened almost out of her wits by Bramforth's words.

"Do not be afraid, my dear, just a slight mishap with the carriage, a small accident, but I thought it would be best if you—"

"Yes, of course. Let us go at once." And she rushed past him, running to the carriage, without a thought of a bonnet or shawl. Williams came hurrying up to the door in time to see her disappear into the coach and Bramforth clamber into the coachman's seat. He whipped up the horses, and they were off before the butler could call after them. Williams stood staring after the carriage for a moment, then stepped back and closed the door slowly, much puzzled at this hurried exit by Miss Sophia, who, he had been informed by Beth, would be expecting the dressmaker at any moment. Back in the kitchen he expiated on the irregularity of young ladies rushing off in gentlemen's carriages, hatless, in what he considered a very ill-behaved way, certainly not what one would expect from Quality, especially when the gentleman in question had no coachman but was driving himself.

Sophia, meantime, was holding onto the squabs to

keep herself from being bounced off the seat as the carriage jolted along over the rough cobblestone streets. Her mind was rushing up to and away from one scene of carnage and horror after another, and she was much too terrified to notice her discomfort, or to have cared if she had. Dear God, she thought, he had not mentioned Augusta. Was it too horrible for him to be able to bring himself to mention? And dear Mallory, would this in any way affect the baby she had just learned about from Augusta? Oh God, oh dear God, why did they not go faster?

Some time had passed before Sophia regained enough awareness to realize that they had been a long time on the way to wherever it was that the mishap had occurred. She looked out the windows, but could see nothing about her that was recognizable. She had been to Cowley's Emporium many times, of course, but she could not remember ever coming through these streets to reach it. Oh—now she remembered that Mallory and Augusta had been going to take up Mrs. Wixton on the way, so perhaps the accident had occured somewhere on the way there, or on the way from Mrs. Wixton's to Cowleys'. Since she had never been to Mrs. Wixton's and had only a hazy idea of where her house was located, she realized that she must just be patient a bit longer.

Another quarter of an hour stretched behind her in achingly slow procession of minutes. Her terror for Mallory and Augusta had abated somewhat, to be replaced by a vague uneasiness and a growing realization of her own acute discomfort as she rattled loosely about alone in the back of the carriage. She moved over to the window and grasped a strap there and stared out to see if she could find some recognizable building or corner, only to realize that the surroundings were thinning out as far as buildings were concerned, and more and more open spaces were making their appearance as they fled down the road. And now, to add to her disquiet, the sound of the wheels on cobblestones changed to the sound of wheels on dirt road. *Good God,* she thought, *we are leaving London! What on earth can be the meaning of this?* She was convinced that nothing could have brought Mallory out this far on such a day as this, with so much still to be done to prepare for the dinner party tonight. And what about that engagement? If Mallory or Augusta was injured in some way, they would have to cancel the dinner party. Well, there was no point in thinking that far ahead at this point. The problem now was to ascertain from Mr. Wixton their direction. She moved over to the opposite seat and knocked on the small window that opened below the coachman's perch. There was no response, so she knocked again, and then again as hard as she could. The carriage continued its headlong pace without pause. She knocked and called as loudly as possible, but received no response at all. Was it possible he could not hear her? She moved to the window, wondering if there was a way to get it open and put her head out to shout at him, but could find no way. Now in a panic, she went back to pound on the coachman's opening, but received nothing for her pains but bruised knuckles. She gave it up and moved back to sit in the middle of the seat, facing forward again, staring wide-eyed first out one side and then the other. They were in open country now, with no visible dwellings to be seen.

Sh went over in her mind the entire course of events leading to her present predicament, but could find no explanation. If the driver had been anyone but Bramforth Wixton, she would have arrived at the obvious explanation much sooner. But she could not equate the portly, sleepy Mr. Wixton with abduction. Unpleasant as he was, he was, after all, a gentleman, and his mother was the very good friend of the duchess. But finally, having thought of and discarded any number of far-fetched explanations, she was left with the inescapable knowledge that this was the only possible one left: Mr. Wixton had indeed abducted her and was now fleeing with her to some unknown destination.

She then remembered that the Wixtons kept no carriage, and wondered that she had not thought of this before. What was Mr. Wixton doing driving about in such a carriage, in any case, without a coachman? Why,

149

just this morning Mallory had received a note from Mrs. Wixton asking to be taken on the shopping expedition, when if their circumstances had changed and they were now able to keep a carriage, why had not Bramforth driven his mother himself?

Perhaps he had borrowed the carriage, and had been on the way to his mother's home, when he had happened upon the Portman carriage accident—oh, fudge, that story was all a hum, she scolded herself, for if it were true, why were they now going so far out into the country? *All right then, I must face the fact that he has borrowed the carriage for just this purpose—to kidnap me. But why should he want to do such an insane thing? I would have thought he would be more likely to kidnap Augusta, if his mind was so bent on kidnapping someone. Unless he was doing this for someone else!*

With this horrible thought, the image of Bruce Coverly rose before her eyes, and she cried aloud. *No, no,* she begged silently, *not him. Dear God, please not that slimy creature!*

She felt the tears begin to slide down her cheeks and caught her breath on a sob, and felt about in the pocket of her gown for a handkerchief. But of course, none was there. *Well,* she thought, with a tiny hiccup of a laugh, *that settles it. I cannot cry since I have no kerchief, and I will* not *stoop to using the hem of my gown. I'll wager Augusta would not cry in such a situation.* Sophia tried to picture her sister in this very seat. What would she do? She would throw herself out of the carriage, if she could not get Mr. Wixton to stop, Sophia felt sure. With this thought in mind, she leaned forward tentatively and tried the handle, only to discover, with some relief, that the door was locked. The relief was because she could not now be forced to make a decision to jump from a moving carriage, which she was not sure she would have the courage for. But after the relief came anger. How dare he lock her into this carriage! This outrage caused her to sit up stiffly, and glare at the unseen figure in the coachman's seat. *Very well, we shall just see* she thought grimly. *At some point he will have to stop, and then it may be possible to contrive some escape from this intolerable situation.*

But as mile followed mile she was forced to lean back in weariness. She had no way of being sure how long she had now been in the carriage, but she could see that the sun had moved from directly overhead and was now edging to the west, so it must be at least two in the afternoon, and if she had lingered at the table for a half-hour after Mallory and Augusta left for their shopping, it would have been close to ten-thirty when Mr. Wixton had come to the door. That meant she had been gone four hours. In any case, they would have returned from their shopping by now, and have had luncheon, and would be just beginning to be perturbed by her own absence.

The thought of them at the luncheon table reminded her suddenly that she had been too nervous to eat anything but a slice of toast at breakfast, and that she was now hungry. She wondered if Mr. Wixton would consider a stop for refreshment. Besides, surely the horses must be wearying and would need to be bated soon.

But it was at least another hour before Bramforth, feeling that they must be far enough out of London to be safe, considered stopping. Apart from the consideration of safety, there was the fact that he was feeling quite faint with hunger himself. If he remembered correctly, there was a good inn, located in the next village, whose roast chicken he had sampled about a year ago. This memory settled things. They must stop there, he decided.

His mouth watering with anticipation, he finally pulled into the innyard and clambered stiffly down from his perch. The ostlers hurried forward to begin unhitching the horses, and the landlord hustled out to greet him. Bramforth immediately ordered a roast chicken to be prepared, and then dealt with the problem of a fresh team of horses, grumbling at the price quoted to him. Everything being put in train, he turned to deal with his captive bride.

He unlocked and opened the coach door, and grinned ingratiatingly at the ramrod-stiff figure sitting inside. He tried to convey a look of schoolboy charm, combined with

151

a look of one who knows he's done wrong but is sure he'll be forgiven. It was all wasted, for the lady continued to stare stonily ahead.

"Dear girl, I know you will forgive my impetuous behavior when you realize the passionate feelings behind it. My heart simply could not withstand another moment without you. I could not—"

"I am not your dear girl," she interrupted in a voice of ice.

"Ah, but you are, you are very dear to me."

"Mr. Wixton, I don't know what you think you are doing, or how you think you can hope to get away with it, but I do assure you my brother will be following us by this time. Also my fiancé."

"Your—" Bramforth was momentarily speechless.

"Fiancé. The Duke of Carnmoor. I believe you are well acquainted with him?"

"But, Miss Portman, surely it is your sister—"

"I am my sister. I mean, I am—oh, for heaven's sakes, I am *not* Miss Portman. I am Miss Sophia Portman!"

Bramforth's jaw fell open, and a look of horror came into his eyes, as he thought of his mother, the duchess, and the Portman family, not to mention Harry. This last name was more frightening than all the rest. *Good God,* he thought, *I might be forced to fight a duel! But—but— I didn't mean—it's all a terrible mistake! I must take her back immediately and explain the whole thing.* It was at this point that the sneering face of Bruce Coverly loomed before him, and he shuddered to think of the tongue-lashing he would have to endure when this blunder reached his ears. Bramforth cast about wildly in his mind for someone to blame besides himself, but there was no one. He remembered clearly Bruce's voice instructing him to ask for "Miss Portman," to make sure he had the right twin, and though he had no memory of exactly what he had said at the Portman door, he had obviously not said the magic words, otherwise this embroglio could not have come about.

Now I must be calm, he told himself, *and try to think what is best to do. What would Coverly do in such a pre-*

dicament? But try as he might, Bramforth, who was almost totally devoid of imagination, could not come up with any idea of what his friend might do in the circumstances.

He tried to think of when the Portman family would have become alarmed by Miss—by Sophia's absence in order to arrive at some conclusion as to his head start. Would they follow in the same road? Should he try to take another route back to London? He rushed into the stables to consult the ostler, and an instant later turned and ran back to the carriage, just as Sophia had begun to step down. He pushed her back into the carriage unceremoniously, slammed the door and turned the latch to lock it. She pounded helplessly on the window. He rushed back to the stable and demanded that a fresh team be put to immediately.

The ostler looked at him in some bewilderment. "But sor, be 'ee not batin' yersils then?"

This brought Bramforth up short as nothing else could have done. He thought of the chicken, even now roasting for his dinner, and abruptly changed his mind.

"Right. We'll eat first, but do you have them harnessed up and waiting in an hour from now."

He went back to the carriage and without a word, hustled Sophia out and into the innkeeper's best private parlor, where a table was set for them and a fire burning in the grate.

"Now, Miss Sophia, we're going to have our lunch, and then I'm going to drive you back to London. However, if you say one word, or make any disturbance of any kind in front of the landlord, I won't do it. I'll keep you here all night and your reputation will be ruined. Now sit you down quietly."

She sat down angrily, her eyes flashing, but made no response of any kind. He took her silence for agreement and sat down at the table to pour himself a glass of wine.

The door opened to admit the beaming landlord, proudly bearing a roasted chicken on a platter, and his wife with a bowl of boiled potatoes and a basket of bread.

When they were between herself and Bramforth, Sophia

153

leaped from her chair and whisked out the open door. She ran out the door of the inn and into the road. Without stopping she sped off down the road, hearing behind her the voice of Bramforth bellowing for her to stop.

Chapter Eighteen

Charles arrived home from his early morning ride to find the house unusually quiet. He rang for Williams, and the butler came immediately.

"I'll have some wine, Williams. All the ladies out shopping?"

"Well, sir, Mrs. Portman and Miss Portman went off to do some errands sometime ago in the carriage. Miss Sophia—er—left not too long after—in a carriage, also."

Before he could explain the strange wording of his remark about Sophia, the knocker was heard and Williams excused himself to go and answer it.

He returned, followed by Courtley, and then went off to fetch the wine for the gentlemen. When he came back, bearing the decanter and two glasses on a tray, Charles immediately resumed their previous conversation.

"Now then, Williams, what the devil did you mean about Miss Sophia before?"

"Well, sir, I'm not sure if I know. Only that it didn't seem right to me, her going off like that."

"Confound it, Williams, come out with it. Going off like what?"

"You see, sir, I was in the pantry, polishing the silver, when the knocker went. I had to fetch my jacket and wipe my hands and—"

"Williams! Stop havering and get to the point!" ordered Charles impatiently.

"Beggin' your pardon, sir, but that is the point," replied Williams, in injured tones. "By the time I got to the door, Miss Sophia was just climbing into the carriage at the curb, and she had no bonnet on!"

Throughout this exchange Courtley, quietly sipping his wine, had not heard anything startling enough to give him pause, but now he raised his eyes in astonishment, for well he knew that no lady would dream of going without a bonnet for a ride in a carriage.

"Whose carriage was it?" asked Charles in surprise.

"Well, I never saw the carriage before, but I'm sure it was Mr. Wixton climbing up into the coachman's seat."

"Mr. Wixton!" exclaimed Charles. "But Wixton doesn't have a carriage."

And Courtley added, "Into the coachman's seat? It was a closed carriage then, was it?"

"Yes, sir, and as I said, Miss Sophia must have answered the door herself before I could get there, and then went off, just as she was, and left no message nor anything, and here's Beth in hysterics in the kitchen, because the seamstress is here to pin up Miss's hem for the dress she's wearing to the party tonight," answered Williams in a much-put-upon voice.

The two gentlemen looked at each other with raised eyebrows for a moment, then turned and continued to ply Williams with questions. But after awhile they were forced to the conclusion that Williams had already told them all he knew. Miss Sophia had answered the door and gone off in a carriage driven by Mr. Wixton without her bonnet and leaving no message for anyone. Beth was called in and questioned but she could add nothing further to the store of information, except to confirm that Miss Sophia was coming up directly after breakfast to meet with the seamstress. Beth showed signs of being ready to burst into tears, so Charles hastily dismissed her.

After a short discussion, Courtley and Charles decided that each would set off in a different direction to try to locate Bramforth Wixton, or anyone who had seen him driving a carriage this morning. Williams was to stay near the front door to await Sophia's return, but in case Mrs. Portman returned before they did, he was to say nothing to her. Neither of the gentlemen had, as yet, any reason to feel alarm at Sophia's disappearance. They agreed it was unlike her to go out without leaving word of her whereabouts, and strange in her to go without a bonnet, but still the explanation could be a quite simple and uncomplicated one.

Charles' destination was to the Wixton house, where he was told by a very depressed-looking maid that neither her master nor mistress was home, and she didn't know where they were. Her manner indicated that neither did she care.

Courtley had gone directly to Bramforth's club, seeking information as to news of the purchase, by Wixton, of a carriage. He could find no one there who could tell him anything, but on St. James Street he had the good fortune to run into Bruce Coverly.

"Ah, Coverly, a word with you, please," said Courtley politely.

Bruce was in high good humor at the success of his scheme for revenge against the Portmans, and was ready enough to stand and chat with Courtley. He had heard rumors that Armstead was dangling after Sophia, and felt that he and Courtley had a great deal in common, now that Sophia's engagement to Lord Carnmoor had been announced. After all, she had spurned both of them, hadn't she?

"Good morning, Armstead. Grand day, isn't it?"

"Yes, lovely. I was wondering if you had seen your friend Wixton this morning?"

"Seen him? Well, yes, I've seen him," Bruce smirked.

"Was he driving a closed carriage when you saw him?"

"Why do you ask?"

"Oh, no reason, really," said Courtley, deciding he had best be very cautious with Bruce, since the latter was Bramforth's best friend and might not care to discuss his friend's affairs with a stranger. Little did he know Bruce! "Friend told me he'd seen Wixton driving a closed carriage this morning, and it occurred to me that he doesn't keep one, and well—just curious, don't you know."

Through this speech Bruce had commenced to snicker, and now he began to laugh in great glee, mystifying Courtley no end.

"Here, what's the joke then?" he asked.

"Oh, a good joke, really. Come to the club tonight, and I'll tell you all about it. Can't tell now, too soon." And again he was seized by gusts of laughter.

"Well, I must say the idea of Wixton's buying a closed carriage and driving it himself is a funny one," said Courtley with a smile.

"Oh, that's not the joke. But I'll say no more now. Spoil everything if I tell too soon. However, he didn't buy that carriage, only borrowed it."

"Borrowed it? How strange then, not to have borrowed the coachman also," replied Courtley, hoping to prod Bruce into further indiscretion.

"Oh, no, couldn't do that. M'friend said he'd let him have the carriage, but needed his coachman."

"Your friend? Oh, I see, your friend lent Wixton the carriage for some lark, is that it? And you'll tell me tonight what it is? Couldn't you just give me the smallest hint? I'll not be able to accomplish anything all day, trying to puzzle it out," coaxed Courtley.

"Well, I'll tell you this much. Wixton's in love!" Bruce clapped Courtley on the back heartily and went off down the street, laughing to himself in great good humor.

Bramforth in love? Yes, Courtley knew he had been pestering Augusta this age, but that didn't explain Sophia rushing out of the house and into his carriage without a word. He decided the best thing was to go back to the

158

Portmans' with this information and hope that Charles had come up with something more promising.

But when they exchanged the news they had gleaned from their expeditions, they could make nothing of it. In the midst of their discussion, Mallory and Augusta arrived, laden with various small packages and agreeing that it had been a most trying morning, with Mrs. Wixton gushing and cooing and making requests for just one more small stop—she was sure they would not mind if she just darted in for a moment.

"Charles, darling, home for lunch? Why, what are you two looking so serious about?" asked Mallory, as she raised herself on tiptoe to kiss her husband.

"Mallory, did you know that Sophia was going out with Bramforth Wixton this morning?"

"Going out with—why, of course she was not. She is upstairs having her gown hemmed for this evening."

"No, darling, she is not upstairs."

"Charlie, don't be silly. Of course she is," interjected Augusta. "Did you check with Beth?"

"Augusta, don't be silly, of course we did," he parroted, "and she is not there. Williams tells me she went out shortly after you left, and that he saw her climbing into a closed carriage driven by Bramforth Wixton and that she was not wearing a bonnet."

"But—but—that doesn't make any sense, Charles. Why should she go anyplace with Bramforth Wixton? And she would not go out without wearing a bonnet," said a bewildered Mallory.

"She might if it were some emergency," said Augusta slowly, trying to make some sense out of the events.

"But what emergency could cause her to go with Bram?" asked Charles. And since this was an unanswerable question they all stood for some moments in silence.

Finally Augusta asked, "This carriage. Whose carriage was it, since we know the Wixtons don't keep one?"

"Oh, I can answer that one," replied Courtley, "I ran into Bruce Coverly, who told me that Bram had borrowed it, and there is some joke about it which he will

159

reveal to me tonight if I come to his club. He would only say that Bram is in love!"

"Yes, but with Augusta, not Sophia!" said Mallory. "Besides, he would never dare to make advances to Sophia, since he knows she is betrothed to Harry. Mrs. Wixton would never allow it. She'd be too afraid it would lose her the duchess' friendship."

"But how if he didn't know it was Sophia?" asked Augusta. "You know yourself how stupid he is. Perhaps he came to the door, and, thinking it was I who answered it, took her along with him."

"Took her along with him where? And why?" interrupted Mallory, her voice rising with anxiety.

"Now, Mal, hysterics won't help and they are not your style in any case. Just be calm and let us all apply our energies to working out this puzzle." Charles soothed her, putting his arm around her shoulders.

"But Charles, the duchess tonight and her dress and—" began Mallory.

"Now, Mallory, you must be calm and help us," reproved Charles. "Let's try to think of why Wixton would have come around here with a closed carriage and persuaded Sophia to go someplace with him."

"I still opt for the emergency story," said Augusta. "It's the only thing that explains her going without a bonnet and without a message. She is much too careful and too thoughtful to have done such a thing for any other reason. I think he came here with some Banbury story, thinking to lure me into going for a drive with him. Now I think of it, he did ask me some time ago if I would, but I put him off."

"I think you're right, Gussie," said Charles. "But what story could he have told her?"

"It had to be something about Mallory and myself. She knew we were going to pick up Mrs. Wixton, so she would have believed him if he said he had come about us. Yes, that must be it! He told her something had happened to us at his mother's or on the way to the stores, some accident perhaps, and she simply rushed out to the carriage without a thought for anything except to come to us."

"That sounds right, but where are they now? What was his purpose in luring her into a car—oh, my God!" exclaimed Mallory, all the color draining from her face, as the possibility came to her. "He is eloping with her!"

A stunned silence followed this dramatic announcement, as they all tried to assimilate the possibility and found it was easily believable. It was just the sort of stupid, insensitive thing they could imagine Bramforth doing, and it was the only likely explanation they could come up with. After a moment they all began talking at once, until finally Charles called them to order.

"Now we must all try to think logically what we must do, and it won't help if we all talk at once. We will go around, and each may speak his piece. Mallory, you begin," he said, knowing that she was on the verge of tears.

"Thank you, darling, but you need not fear. I am going to be sensible. The thing is, of course, someone must go after them immediately. And then there is the very pressing problem of the duchess and what we are to do about that situation. Should we take Harry into our confidence and see if he can help? Oh, I can't think. Someone else speak, please." She subsided suddenly onto the sofa, but then sat up very stiffly, willing herself to be calm.

"I think I must go after them immediately, and I will order my horse brought round at once. I can go faster on horseback than in a carriage." And Charles headed for the door to call for Williams.

"But Charles, what of the dinner party? What shall we do? Shall I send a note to say Sophia is indisposed?" asked Mallory.

"Good God, Mallory," responded Augusta, "how can we do so at this late hour? She would have to try to notify all her guests not to come. And think of all the preparations she must have gone through!"

"Yes, but they were for Sophia. It will hardly do to go to the party without the bride-to-be!" wailed Mallory.

"I—I—now, Mallory, hear me out before you say anything. I know this sounds dreadful, but how if I went as Sophia, and we said Augusta had come down with a fever or a headache or something?"

"Oh, Augusta, we could not, it would be dishonorable to perpetrate such a hoax on that nice old lady," protested Mallory.

"I think it might be justified, in this case," said Courtley. "After all, if word of this gets out, it will ruin Sophia's reputation. No one will believe she could have gone unwillingly into Bram's carriage, or, at least there will always be suspicions."

"But surely no one would think that a girl engaged to Carnmoor would *willingly* elope with Bramforth Wixton!" said Mallory.

"There are always people who enjoy wagging their tongues to someone's discredit, especially if the person is beautiful and fortunate. They like to see those luckier than themselves have a comedown," said Courtley.

"Yes, you are right," said Mallory, still doubtfully, "but Augusta and I can hardly go alone. If Charles is going after them—"

"I will go after them!" declared Courtley. "I was preparing to accompany Charles, in any case. It cannot be any secret to anyone here how I feel about Sophia. She is dearer to me than—well, never mind. But I will be very happy to come face to face with that scum Wixton!" he said savagely.

Mallory and Charles both began to object, but Augusta interrupted them firmly.

"He is right. He will go after them, then Charlie and you, Mallory, will take me, as Sophia. Then all the most important people will be there. And besides, it will be much less confusing to the duchess' guests!" She ended with an unhappy attempt to laugh.

They spent another ten minutes arguing the point, but finally all conceded that in the circumstances it was the best plan that could be devised. Mallory still protested the repugnance she felt at playing such a trick on the Carnmoors. Charles still protested that he wanted to go after the dastardly Wixton. But, in the end, realizing that they were wasting precious time, the group adopted the plan. Without ceremony, Courtley took his leave and ran out to throw himself into the saddle of Charles' waiting horse. Mallory and Augusta went off upstairs to placate the seamstress and have Sophia's gown hemmed, and Charles, feeling enraged and helpless, poured himself another glass of wine.

Chapter Nineteen

*Sophia, her gown hoisted almost to her knees in a most un-*ladylike way, rounded a curve in the road, running as fast as her legs would carry her. She spotted a break in the hedge, and, without hesitation, leapt the gully beside the road and spurted across an open field into the shelter of a copse of trees. When she felt their welcome cover begin to close around her, she stopped, completely winded, and sank to the ground to catch her breath. She heard the sound of shouting and held her gasping breath to listen, her heart pounding. That was Bramforth, still calling for her to stop, and she heard his heavy, running footsteps pounding on down the road, past the break in the hedge. But she wasn't safe yet. She knew that eventually he would came to an open stretch of road and find she was no longer on it. Then he would turn back and begin searching along the sides, and surely he would not miss the break in the hedge, an obvious place for her to have left the road—as this copse was an obvious place to hide, she suddenly realized. She crept back to the beginning of the woods and peered out, but could think of no place better within sight. Where would he not search?

Across the field, through the break in the hedge, she could see the road, and across the road another hedge. He would not look on that side, because there was no break. Without pausing to give herself time to think and perhaps become afraid to act, she sped back across the field, hesitated at the road to be sure he was not in sight, and darted across the road and straight at the dense hedge on the other side. She went down on all fours, and wriggling and pushing blindly, ignoring the tearing and scratching, shoved her way through, and froze, just on the other side as she heard his footsteps and heavy panting coming back down the road.

She cowered down and peering through the branches saw Bramforth pause at the break in the hedge, then resolutely slide down the gully and clamber up the other side and start across the field. Presently he disappeared into the copse of trees. She looked about herself and saw another open field. But there in the middle was a large spreading elm tree. She looked back to make sure Bramforth was still in the woods, then ran across to the tree, and, without hesitation, hiked her skirts up and tucked them under the band of her bloomers and leaped for the lowest branch. She swung for a second, then threw up her leg and hoisted herself onto the branch. She sat there, glowing with triumph that she could still accomplish this tomboyish feat. She and Augusta had spent a great deal of time climbing trees when they were younger, before Mallory came to take them in hand. Sophia reached for the branch above her and carefully stood up. Then she began to climb higher, until she found a comfortable angle of branch and trunk, where she finally rested, feeling certain that she was perfectly secure, even if Bramforth should come into this field. It would never occur to him to look for her in the tree, for the simple reason that it would never occur to him that she was capable of climbing it.

Bramforth, after searching the copse fruitlessly, came back to the road and made his way dispiritedly back to the inn. He was much too tired to search further. He would go back to the inn, eat his, by now, cold chicken, and have several tankards of ale, then request a room for a short nap. By his calculations he had no need to feel pressed for time, for he felt sure Sophia would not have been seen leaving the house and would not even be missed for some hours after lunch. Perhaps by now—what was it, a bit past three?—they would begin to wonder where she had gone, and in another hour or so, if she hadn't returned, they would begin to worry. Why, he had several hours before he need bestir himself. And if they did come to the inn, he would be long gone.

Damn and blast that little baggage, anyway. If she had only waited until he had eaten, he would have taken her back to London. And so he would tell anyone who dared to accuse him of not behaving properly. He had never had any other thought in his mind but to return her when he had discovered his mistake, and it was her own fault if she refused to believe the word of a man of honor, and hared off like that. Serve her right if she had to walk all the way back to London!

Having thus justified himself, he trudged wearily into the inn and his long-postponed luncheon, never suspecting that his nemesis was over halfway to the inn at that very moment.

Sophia's white dress had been hemmed and was now spread across her bed, waiting for Augusta. Mallory, unable to bring herself to leave Augusta, was pacing back and forth across the room, her hands twisted together until the knuckles were white.

"This will never work," she proclaimed. "They will catch you out. And think of Harry—he has always been able to tell you apart."

"He tells us apart by our voices and by the way we speak, as anyone could who took the trouble. But I assure you, darling Mal, I am well enough acquainted with my twin to imitate her perfectly. Please calm yourself and go along and dress."

Augusta tried to speak quietly and positively, for she knew Mallory was jumping with nerves. Not only from the ordeal that faced them, but with worry about Sophia. Augusta was also worried about Sophia, but somehow she could not be as up in the boughs as Mallory. She knew Bramforth would not hurt Sophia in any way, and she had every confidence that Courtley would catch up with them and deal with Bramforth and bring Sophia safely back. Where this confidence came from, she could not know, but it was there. Her real worry was with herself, and how she would be able to face Harry, trying to be a sweet and yielding Sophia, and yet not allow any real intimacy. She could not in honor allow him to touch her, now that he was betrothed to her sister. And yet she knew it would be torment to be so close to him, so longing for the sweetness that could only be Sophia's, and that, playing the part of Sophia, she should allow his presence and yet must resist. Was anyone ever in such a difficult and terrible situation? she wondered.

She sat down at her dressing table for Beth to begin brushing and arranging her hair. Mallory came over to watch for a moment, and then, realizing the lateness of the hour, forced herself to go and begin her own preparations. Augusta was left looking blankly into the mirror, her mind touching lightly on imagined scenes coming up for her with the duchess and Harry, and how she would play them. She finally put them aside, unable to bear the thought of them anymore. *I must just do it*, not think about it, she decided.

Now she began to think of Sophia, jolting along the road somewhere, alone and frightened, and reached out to her with her thoughts. *Be brave, little one, Courtley is coming*, she said over and over to the image of Sophia's face before her eyes.

The ordeal began. The carriage swept up to the townhouse of the Carnmoors', and deposited the Portmans. They were received and led into the drawing room, almost before Augusta had to time to realize what was happening to her. Now, when she needed her wits about her as never before in her life, she felt herself to be in a strange, dreamlike state, as though she were walking under water. The walk across the floor to the duchess seemed to take an eternity, the faces of the other guests were only blurs, and all sound receded for a moment.

"My dear, how very beautiful you are looking tonight," said a voice, the one voice that could reach her in this state, and she turned dazed eyes to find Harry at her side, his hands enclosing her own warmly. Everything clicked back into place instantly, and she smiled enchantingly up at him for a moment, then dropped her eyes, just as she knew Sophia would have done.

"Thank you, Harry," she said demurely, pressing his hand very slightly in return, and then pulling it away gently. She turned to the duchess and curtseyed, and then bent to kiss her cheek.

"Dear girl, how very nice. And Harry is right, you are radiant tonight. Now come." She struggled up and out of her chair and took Augusta by the arm. "All these dear people are eager to meet you."

She was led around the room and introduced to at least thirty people, whose names she was never after able to recall. But they all smiled kindly upon her, and made her feel that they were, indeed, eager to make her acquaintance. Then she found herself being led into dinner by Harry, immediately behind Charlie with the duchess on his arm, and followed by Mallory and a courtly old gentleman.

The dinner table seemed to stretch for miles, brilliant with white brocade, crystal and silver, and gleaming with candlelight. She was never able to remember exactly what she put into her mouth that night, so engrossed was she with the role she was playing.

Harry was all kindness and attentiveness, bending solicitously toward her every utterance. His nearness, his warmth, very nearly undid her in the beginning. He had reached over and taken her hand in his for a moment.

"My dear, I hope that you are not being made in any

way uneasy by all these eyes upon you. It is all most kindly meant, I assure you," he said, smiling gently at her.

"No. No, of course not, Harry. They are all lovely. There are—quite a lot of them, however. Are they relatives?"

"Some. You'll get them all sorted out another time. Don't worry about it now. Tell me, how is Augusta? It is nothing serious, I hope?" His tone, just a shade too casual, sounded unlike him, and she darted him a glance. He was staring directly at her very intently, waiting for her answer.

"Why—no. Only the headache," she said hastily, turning away her head. "She was devastated to have to miss this evening."

Had she not turned away, she would have seen the tension go out of him at her words, and wondered why he should have been so concerned.

"Mrs. Portman seems somewhat—er—distraught tonight," he continued, "but I suppose she is worrying about your sister."

"Yes, she certainly is!" said Augusta in such a forthright tone of voice, so entirely different than she had used before, that now it was his turn to stare at her. She realized her mistake and tried to cover. "Mallory is much given to fretting over both of us. Charlie is forever teasing her about it." She ended with a gay little laugh and a flash of dimples.

"It is natural that she should, I suppose, while you are in her charge. But soon she will have one less to worry about, at least. And then I imagine—" he hesitated for a moment and cleared his throat, "your sister, too, will be leaving her charge soon."

"Leaving her charge?"

"Well, what I mean is, that of course she will be married before long—I should imagine."

"Why, no, of course she will not be!" protested Augusta, with more vehemence than she was aware of.

He looked startled for a moment. "But, my dear Sophia, of course she will be. She is a beautiful girl, just as you

170

are, and there are many young men dangling after her already."

"There is no one."

"And what of Hampton Madderson? I feel quite sure there is a great deal of feeling between them from what I have observed."

"Oh, well, Mr. Madderson is—no, you are wrong, she does not love him," said Augusta positively—too positively for Sophia to be saying, she realized belatedly, and tried to recover. "At least, I feel sure it cannot be so, or she would have told me."

"I see. Well." He could think of nothing to say. His mind was rejoicing in the news, while the stern voice of conscience told him he had no business to be rejoicing, and furthermore it was dishonorable of him to be questioning sweet, innocent Sophia in this way. But he could no more have helped himself than the tongue can stop probing a sore tooth.

Augusta became aware that her partner on the other side had turned to her and was patiently waiting for her attention, and she turned to him with relief. She knew that Harry's questions had nearly caused her to betray herself, and sternly reminded herself what she was supposed to be doing here tonight. *We are here to save our darling Sophia's reputation,* she told herself, *and if I cannot control myself enough to accomplish that, then it is even more dishonorable to perpetrate this hoax on these good people.* Strengthened by this lecture, she was able to perform her role perfectly the rest of the evening.

After the gentlemen rejoined the ladies in the drawing room, several of the young ladies performed on the pianoforte, and Augusta managed one of Sophia's favorite ballads with great aplomb and to much applause.

The only moment that spoiled the perfect performance was as they were waiting in the hall for their cloaks. Harry was saying good night to a lady and Augusta was talking to the duchess. He turned and called "Sophia," and Augusta went on speaking to the duchess, without turning around or even realizing that he had spoken. He called her name again.

The duchess, giving her a puzzled look, said, "My dear, Harry seems to be addressing you."

"What? Harry? Oh—" She turned to him in some confusion. "Forgive me, Harry, I didn't hear you." And she blushed.

Harry, while accustomed to Sophia's blushes, watched with astonishment as the furious color swept up Augusta's neck and across her face. Sophia usually blushed gently, and dropped her eyes in confusion. This time she raised her chin and stared at him belligerently as though willing the blush not to be, or defying him to see it. What on earth—?

He came across to take her hand again. "My dear, is anything wrong?"

She shook her head mutely, and her hand began to tremble slightly in his.

"Lady Hargreaves is making up a party for a picnic on Monday, if the weather holds fine, and wondered if we would join them. Would that please you?"

Augusta managed to unclench her jaw, and she swallowed and smiled bravely up at him.

"Oh, a picnic! It is what I like of all things!"

He patted her hand and turned away to speak to Lady Hargreaves again, and Augusta turned back to the duchess.

"My child, I am very worried about your dear sister. I will send around tomorrow to inquire, and if there is anything I can do, I know you will be good enough to tell me," said the duchess.

"You are very kind, Your Grace, but I assure you there is no need for concern. It is just the headache, and we are confident all will be well by morning," Augusta replied.

"You must take every care, since I have found that often a headache is a presage of something more serious." The duchess leaned forward and lowered her voice. "As soon as Lady Hargreaves leaves—she does tend to talk on forever—I will say good night and slip away myself. I'm sure you will want a private moment with Harry."

"Oh, please do not—I mean—it is quite all right, Your Grace, we—I—" she floundered helplessly.

172

"Now, now, my dear, I was young once myself, though you may find that hard to believe, looking at me now. But I was, and I know how much lovers need a few moments alone."

Augusta tried to look grateful, but her feeling was one of panic. The last thing she wanted at this point was a private moment with Harry. But surely Mallory and Charlie would not desert her. She looked around to find that the duchess was going up to them and leaning forward to say something quietly to them, and knew she was suggesting they wait in the carriage for a few moments in order to give Sophia and Harry a moment alone. She saw Mallory flash a worried look at her, but knew that Mallory would be unable to do anything to help her. The duchess was even now gently urging them to the door, and they were unable to resist her. Mallory threw one more speaking glance over her shoulder, and then she and Charlie were out the door on the heels of Lady Hargreaves. The duchess turned triumphantly, gave Augusta a wink of understanding and complicity, and marched firmly up the stairs to her room.

Harry turned from the door, the butler discreetly disappeared, and they were alone. As Harry advanced toward her, Augusta could feel the trembling begin in her knees and hands and could do nothing to stop it.

"My mother is a scheming old thing, is she not? And not too subtle, I fear," he said, taking both her hands in his own and smiling down at her. "Why what is this, Sophia? Your hands are trembling! Has the evening been such an ordeal?"

"I could more easily have fought a duel," she admitted frankly.

"Why, how silly you are. There was absolutely no need for nerves tonight. After all, these people are practically family, and all wish you well."

"Yes, you are right, I am being silly," she said with a shaky little laugh.

He tilted her chin with his finger so that she was forced to look at him, then very gently and softly kissed her lips before she had time to fully realize what he was doing. She felt herself melting, and without conscious volition, kissed him back. His arms went about her, and pulled her close, and for one passionate moment they were entirely lost. Then she realized what she was doing and pushed him away violently and they stood staring at one another in confusion. She gasped an incoherent speech of apology and good night, and, snatching up her wrap, jerked open the front door and fled to the waiting carriage.

Harry watched her go, still unable to make any move or think of what to say. His mind was filled with a jumble of flashing, disconnected thoughts, and it was some moments after the door closed behind her before he was able to pull himself together enough to think.

The first thought to emerge was a straight and simple statement of fact. "That was Augusta!" And no matter what arguments he could make to himself that he could not be right, his conviction could not be shaken. He walked slowly into the library, poured himself a glass of port, and sat down before the fire. He sifted carefully through every word of conversation between them during the evening, every impression garnered, searching for clues.

Her continually pulling away from him all evening, what of that? Though Sophia was never in any way forward in initiating physical contact, she never repulsed him either. True, they had not progressed to passionate embraces, but still—this evening however, she had consistently avoided contact as much as possible.

Then, once or twice, he had been puzzled by a difference in the tone of voice and thought at the time she sounded very like Augusta, which was not so wonderful since they were, after all, identical twins, but still—

There was the violent reaction when he had called to her in the hall, and she did not respond immediately, almost as though she were not used to answering to the name of Sophia. Of course, she had been in conversation with his mother, and might just not have heard, but still—

Then he came to the moment he had been postponing, the better to savor it, he realized. He closed his eyes, and felt again the delicate touch of her lips as he thought he was kissing Sophia, and after only the briefest of instants, the flash of fire as she had responded and they had both been swept away. In that moment he had known with absolute conviction that he was kissing Augusta, and now, remembering, there was no voice to say 'but still. . . .'

It *was* Augusta! There was no doubt in his mind on that score, but why it should have been Augusta, pretending to be Sophia at the party tonight, made no sense. If Sophia had been indisposed, there could still have been no need for this elaborate masquerade, and he could not imagine such people as the Portmans, without very good cause, being part of such a trick. Harry wondered if it were possible that his mother had caught on. But no, he thought, that was not possible. She would have said something to him if she had.

His thoughts went around and around, but the more he thought of it the less sense he could make of it. He decided he would say nothing, feeling confident that one of the girls would finally tell him what it had all been about. They were both too open and honest not to feel the need to confess sooner or later. He would wait. Meanwhile, he leaned back and closed his eyes again, and relived that exquisite moment without guilt. It might turn out to be the only one he would ever have with Augusta, and he must make very sure he never forgot it.

enough rest, but that the poor child was certainly would
under her dress.

Harry, nearly frantic with anxiety for Arnold and

Chapter Twenty

Courtley, had, after only a moment's indecision, headed directly for the North, feeling sure Bramforth would go to Gretna Green. If they had left sometime close to ten-thirty, and it was now but one-thirty, they had only three hours' start, and they were driving in a carriage, while he was able to move much more quickly on horseback. He had only to go without stopping, keeping a sharp eye at every inn along the way, in case they had stopped for a change of horses or refreshments, and he would catch them up before they could get too far. His few meetings with Bramforth had convinced him that that gentleman was very fond of his food, and would be unable to go without a meal for too long.

He stopped twice to rest and water his horse, but other than that had an uneventful journey, the horse covering the miles faster than even he would have believed possible. He had passed several inns, but had not seen a stationary carriage in any of the innyards, and so had not had to stop to investigate. He also passed several carriages on the road, but not any with Bramforth driving. Besides, he felt sure it was too soon yet to come up with them. Another hour and he would have to start watching very carefully.

Sophia, though she stood and changed positions as often as possible, was still beginning to feel the discomfort of the branch upon which she was seated. She was unable to relax, for fear that she might fall asleep and tumble out of the tree. She was watching over the hedge for the sight of Bramforth, driving back to London, and could not imagine what he could possibly be doing in the inn for so long. Why, he must have been over an hour by now, surely long enough for him to have eaten his dinner and be ready to start back. She had no intention of coming down from the tree until she had seen him safely away. She had decided that she would then go back to the inn and ask them to drive her back. Surely they kept some sort of conveyance she could hire, and Charlie would pay them when they reached home. She stood up to stretch her cramped body, and peered toward the road again. Drat the man, why did he not finish and leave? It must be close to five in the afternoon, by her calculations, for the sun was making very long shadows now, and the air had lost the warmth of the beautiful spring day. Heavens, what if he decided to spend the night here? Would she be able to spend the whole night in the tree? But then, if he did do such a thing, she could of course come down at least into the field to rest. Though the thought of a night spent alone in this open field, with no wrap of any kind, was daunting. Surely someone would come for her by then, in any case, she thought in anguish. They *must* have missed her by now, and would . . . would what? she wondered. How would they know where to come for her? She had left no message. There had been no one in the hall to see her go. Why, they would never come for her, she thought with a chill of dismay. There was no way they could know to come here seeking her. *Well then, when it is dark, and if it seems that Mr. Wixton is staying the night, then I will just start walking back myself. I could get quite a way along toward London before daylight, and surely I will pass another inn where I can seek help.* This decided, she settled back into her branch, only to come up standing an instant later at the sound of hoofbeats coming along the road. That was a lone rider, and making quite good time too, she noted, and peered impatiently for a glimpse of him, but he was still behind the next curve.

Then horse and rider burst into her sight, and she gave such a start she nearly fell out of the tree. Dear God, that looked like Courtley! *Wait . . . wait,* she cautioned herself. *Don't become too hopeful.* But as he came closer she saw that it was, and she began calling and waving and crying all at the same time, but the horse sped past unheeding.

"Courtley! Wait! See, I am here. Courtley!" But he flashed past and was gone around the bend that led to the inn. She began scrambling down any which way, adding more scratches and rips to her already damaged arms and knees and skirt. She ran blindly across the field, crying and whispering, "Wait. Oh, please wait, Courtley.

Courtley slowed a bit to take in the innyard, and then pulled up his horse so suddenly it almost toppled over backwards. For there, sitting unattended and with empty shafts, was a closed carriage. He trotted into the yard and dismounted, to peer into the carriage windows, but could discover nothing. The ostler came hustling out to take his horse.

"Whose carriage is that?" Courtley inquired.

"Quality from Lunnon, sir."

"Where is he?"

"Inside having a lie-down. Sore spent he were, from chasing atter the wench."

Courtley froze, then grabbed the man's arm before he could walk his horse off to the stables for a rubdown.

"What wen—lady? What do you mean? Why was he chasing her? Where did she go?"

" 'Ere, no call to go shaking me arm like you'd take

179

it off. I was telling ye. The gent'man came with this 'ere lady, and they was inside to the table, when all of sudden, out she comes and off down the road, and him atter her. Then, times, back 'ee comes, alone and goes inside to have his bird and a rest."

"But what happened to the lady?"

"Dunno, I'm sure. Got me own work to do. Can't go rushing about chasing wen—ladies," he amended, after a look at the scowl on Courtley's face.

But the scowl was not for the lad. Courtley let him go, with orders to rub down the horse carefully and feed him, then turned grimly to the inn.

The front parlor was empty and he marched across to the door at the side and opened it on the remains of a meal and an empty room. Although he could hear voices coming from the kitchen quarters, he ignored them and went up the narrow stairs to the second floor. He opened the first door and there, snoring mightily was Bramforth Wixton, boots and jacket discarded, and waistcoat unbuttoned to release his spreading stomach.

Courtley marched over to the bed, seized a jug of water sitting on the table beside it and without hesitation dashed the entire pitcher of water into Bramforth's face. He snored, gasped, cried out and then sat up, to find Courtley glaring at him. He stared back at him blankly, unable for some moments to realize where he was, why he was soaking wet, and what this—Armstead, was it?— was doing here looking at him as though he were ready to kill him.

"What the devil—" He finally found his voice. "What do you mean, sir? What are you doing here? Did you— did you throw water over me?" he asked in amazement, staring down at his ruined waistcoat and shirt.

"Yes, I did, and if you will but stand up, I am hopeful of doing a great deal more to you than that."

"Why, how dare you, sir? I'll call you out for this," blustered Bramforth.

"Don't think for one moment I would dishonor myself by fighting a duel with you, you dog. Now, where is she?"

"Where—" Bramforth stopped, and a look of horror

came into his eyes, as the whole wretched afternoon came back to him and he realized that Courtley was referring to Sophia Portman.

"Yes, where is she? And quick about it, sir. I vow if I have to ask you again, you will be very sorry for it." And Courtley started forward threateningly.

"Now, see here." Bramforth scrambled backward across the bed in a most undignified way. "You'll do no good by talking to me in that tone of voice, Armstead. I will be happy to tell you the whole story, and then you will see that it was all an honest mistake.'"

"A mistake! You call such a dastardly act as abduction a mistake? I'll have the law on you if anything has happened to her, do you hear me? *Now, where is she?*"

"Well, she ran away. And don't threaten me, for it was not my fault. I'd told her I would drive her back to London as soon as I'd eaten. But she doesn't listen and goes tearing off and I searched everywhere for her."

Courley listened to this story with a growing rage that finally threatened to overcome him. He turned away, to try to get himself in hand before he obeyed his impulse to begin thrashing Bramforth with his riding whip.

"Now, let me get this straight," he said finally, turning back to the cowering Bramforth. "You say she ran away and you searched for her. Which way did she run?"

"Why, back down the road toward London. I nearly ran my legs off trying to catch her up, but she just plain disappeared. I finally had to give it up and come back here to wait."

But Courtley had heard enough. He turned on his heel and ran down the stairs and out into the road, and just kept running. The road curved up ahead, and as he sped along, he thought, *If I were Sophia, that is where I would have gone to earth, out of sight of anyone following. Just past there, I must slow down and begin to look about carefully.* But there was no need for him to do so after all, for there, just coming around the bend, was Sophia, racing along at a dead run. They both stopped short for an instant, then continued to run, until she ran straight into his arms. She was sobbing and gasping on his shoulder, and he held her close and murmured into her hair that all would be well now, she was safe.

Finally she raised her tearstained face and asked for his handkerchief, with a little hiccuppy laugh. He gave it to her, and she mopped her eyes and blew her nose and then stood back a pace, but not leaving the circle of his arms. He looked down at her in dismay. Her face was dirty from thrusting through dusty hedges and climbing trees, her hair was coming down in all directions, there were scratches on her arms and her skirt was rent in several places. But she smiled, suddenly and brilliantly.

"I outfoxed him good, didn't I, Courtley?"

He moaned and then snatched her back against his chest and held her tightly. She raised her head again after a moment, looking at him inquiringly, and without thinking he bent to kiss the sweet mouth so temptingly near his own.

"Oh, Courtley," she gasped after a moment, drawing away to look at him in amazement. Then she shut her eyes and reached her arms up to pull his mouth back to hers.

Presently, arms about each other, they started back to the inn, in a wordless daze.

The sight of Bramforth standing in the doorway brought them back to their senses and Sophia dropped her arm from about Courtley's waist, though he kept his about her as he lead her into the innyard, ignoring Bramforth completely. Courtley ordered the ostler to harness fresh horses to the carriage, and asked if there was anyone there who would care to drive the carriage back to London. The ostler went to fetch the landlord, and soon all was arranged. The landlord himself would drive them back, and then return with his horses. Courtley told him that he would send his own groom out the next day to pick up Charles' horse, and meantime could a basin of warm water be carried up to one of the bedrooms, so that the young lady could freshen herself before the trip back?

The landlord's wife came to hustle Sophia upstairs, assuring Courtley that a bite of supper could be laid for them if they would not mind cold beef and bread and butter. After Sophia had washed her face and fastened her hair back up as best she could, they ate their cold beef and were soon ready to leave.

Throughout all this, Bramforth had stayed well out of the way in the front parlor, in a corner by the fire. But now, seeing the carriage being made ready for departure, he came out into the innyard.

"Here, Armstead, that is my carriage, you know. I shall need to get back to London also. I will be happy, of course, to offer you both seats in my carriage.'"

"Wixton, you may go to the devil, for all I care," replied Courtley with gritted teeth. "But one thing for sure, *we* are taking the carriage, and *you* are not coming with us."

"But see here, you can't do that. Why, why—surely you don't mean to go off and leave me here. I'll not allow it!"

"I don't believe you will have any choice," said Courtley, turning his back on Bramforth and handing Sophia up into the carriage. Just before he climbed in himself, he turned again to Bramforth.

"Oh, by the way, I hope no word of this ever gets out. For if it does, I shall know that you have spoken of it and I shall come and thrash you within an inch of your worthless life. And you might just pass that word along to your friend, Coverly, also." And with that he stepped into the carriage and the landlord closed the door after him and climbed up into his own seat and they were away, leaving an outraged Bramforth standing there.

For some time, as the carriage sped down the road in the warm spring dusk, there was silence. Sophia had hardly been conscious of anything that had happened to her since Courtley had kissed her. Her whole being was focused on that one blindingly revelatory moment.

In her head she kept repeating, *I love him, I love him, I love him,* followed by a litany of *And he loves me!*

Courtley, having taken care of the practical matters, was now free to turn his mind also to that happy moment in the roadway, and the way it had felt when her arms had come up to pull his head back down for another kiss. He glanced at her, wondering if this silence meant that she had had second thoughts, and had realized that it was only her gratitude that had caused her to behave so with him. Perhaps she had only been so happy to be rescued. . . .

Sophia reached out at this point and took his hand, and he turned to her, trying to see the expression on her face in the twilight.

"Sophia, before—I hope you did not think I was taking advan—"

"Oh, Courtley, how can you say so? Surely you felt— you knew that I—".

"Sophia, my darling, I must tell you, I love you. I've loved you since the day we met, I think."

"Do you really, Courtley? Then I must tell you also. I love you. And it's not butterflies at all! It's like—like— oh—soaring somehow—oh, how could I not have known."

Here it became necessary for Courtley to sweep her into his arms again and kiss her, and they forgot about the carriage and the night around them and soared.

When they were finally able to look about them again, Sophia suddenly remembered something.

"Good God, Courtley, the Duchess' party! And—and —" her voice died away as she thought of all the "ands."

"Yes. And Harry," Courtley finished her sentence unhappily. They looked at each other for a while in dismay.

"Well, there is no help for it. I don't like to hurt him, when he has been so kind to me always, but it would be worse to marry him loving someone else. I shall just have to ask him to release me from our engagement. It is as well that I didn't get to go to the party tonight and meet all the relatives and friends of—"

"Oh my God!" exclaimed Courtley. "But you did go to the party!"

"I did—what can you mean, Courtley?"

And so he told her of the plan the Portmans had evolved to save her reputation and keep the duchess and Harry from finding out what had happened, while she listened to him in horror. But then her imagination took over and she began to see the funny side of it.

"Oh, Courtley, what an awful tangle we have made of

everything, you loving me and not telling me, me thinking because I had butterflies it must mean I was in love with Harry, Augusta pretending to be me, oh, we have all been stupid. But it is funny." And she began to giggle, and soon he could not help laughing also. Then they began to plan what they should do. Sophia asked that nothing be said to anyone until she had had an opportunity to speak to Harry alone, and Courtley agreed that it was the honorable thing to do. And so they rode back to London, holding hands, planning beyond the tangle of now.

Chapter Twenty-one

*The Portman household was late in rising the next morn-*ing. There had been no bed for any of them till well past midnight. The three who had made up the party to the Carnmoors had arrived back home to find that Courtley and Sophia were still not back, and had spent an anxious hour waiting. Finally there was the sound of hoofbeats, and they had all rushed to the front hall.

Almost before the carriage had stopped, Sophia came tumbling out and ran up the steps into a wildly confused family embrace, while Courtley dealt with the driver. Then they were both swept into the library.

Sophia and Courtley were unusually elated, both laughing and talking at once, but their high spirits were accepted by the rest as a natural outcome of the success of their adventure. Sophia was finally prevailed upon to begin at the beginning, and told them of her ride alone in the carriage, and how Bramforth had persuaded her to come, and then of her escape from him at the inn, and triumphantly, of climbing the tree. She described her long wait there and of seeing Courtley come galloping down the road, and of her fear that he would not stop at the inn and she would lose him, and of running down the road. Then she stopped abruptly, blushed and laughed, and said that was her story, and did it not sound like a novel?

Then Mallory told of their evening at the Carnmoors, while Augusta stared into the fire, unable to speak of it at all. But in the general excitement of the evening it was not noticed. Finally, Courtley took his leave, and the Portmans climbed wearily to their beds.

Now belatedly gathered at the breakfast table they were enjoying the blessedness of being all together, with all anxieties banished. Or so it seemed on the surface. But Augusta was feeling less than tranquil. She had been the last of the family to fall asleep the night before, and had heard the clock from the church towers chiming three in the morning before she finally drifted off.

She had carefully held off the memory of that moment with Harry all through the carriage ride home and the happy reunion that followed. But as soon as the candles were blown out and her head was on her pillow, she was helpless to stop it. She experienced again that joyous falling away of flesh and bone, and the ecstasy of awareness of every blood vessel in her body coursing electrically with excitement. But having allowed this rapturous remembrance, she experienced such shaming guilt that she nearly woke Sophia to confess all. Naturally she did not, realizing at the same time that while it would afford her some relief, it would put a burden upon Sophia that would spoil her happiness in her forthcoming marriage. *I must just live with it,* she thought, *and pray that I will never again so betray her—or myself, and be grateful that Harry will never guess.*

When they had all been served and the servants had withdrawn, Charlie cautioned all of them about discussing the past evening's events with each other in the presence of the servants.

188

"But Charles, Williams must surely know already some of what happened," protested Mallory.

"I will tell him of it myself, it's only fair, but you may be sure that not a word of it will be passed on to the rest of the staff. Now what about Beth?"

Augusta assured him that he need have no fears on that score, that Beth would rather die than do anything to harm them.

They all heard the front-door knocker at the same time, and looked up with varying degrees of expectation. Sophia jumped up and started for the door.

"Oh, I do hope that is Harry," she said eagerly, "I must speak to him."

But Williams came in before she reached the door to announce Mr. Madderson to see Miss Portman. Augusta rose slowly and placed her napkin carefully on the table, her mind full of the sight of Sophia's happy face when she had thought it was Harry come to call. She could not know that Sophia, now that she knew the truth about her feelings, could hardly wait to confess them to Harry.

Hampton came forward quickly to take Augusta's hand, as she came into the drawing room.

"My dear, I hope you will forgive the earliness of this call, but after a sleepless night, I realized that if I was ever to have peace I would have to speak to you immediately. Will you allow me to speak?"

Augusta looked at him silently for a long moment while a whole life flashed in front of her eyes. A life of peace and—safety—with this good person, away from the temptation to betray herself as she had the night before. She saw them married and making a life together, with children and a home and new friends. But then she wondered if it would be fair to do such a thing to him? Would her feelings for Harry die eventually if she became involved in a totally new and different life? Would she be able to love Hampton? *Of course I will,* she thought; *after all, I like him so well already, and under the steady benison of his love, mine will grow.*

"Yes," she said finally, hoping her face was expressing gladness and not resignation, "you may speak."

"Augusta! My darling, thank you. I have loved you since first I saw you, I believe. I want, more than anything in the world, to marry you and have you for my own forever. Is it possible that you will say yes?"

"I must tell you, Mr. Madderson, that, much as I wish it were not so, I cannot say that I have fallen in love with you. I like you very much, as I think you must know, and I—"

He clasped her shoulders with his strong hands, interrupting her speech, "Say no more, my love, it isn't necessary. I am aware that your feelings are not so strongly involved as my own, but I have every confidence that they will grow to match mine. I love you so much, you see," he said with such a sweet smile that Augusta felt her heart turn over, "and I have only one request to make. No, I have two requests."

"What, Mr. Madderson?"

"That you will marry me and that you will call me Hampton," he replied with a laugh.

"I will marry you, Hampton," she answered simply.

"Augusta!" he breathed, and folded her crushingly in his arms.

After a moment she gasped and pulled away. "Sir, I beg you, have pity on my poor ribs, I fear they will be broken," she said lightly.

"If I promise to exert extreme care, may I be allowed to kiss you?" he asked.

In answer, she raised her mouth and closed her eyes—and felt nothing. Though her mind commanded her that having said "yes" she must give wholeheartedly, she could not obey. *Not yet,* she pleaded with her stern voice of conscience, *I will, I promise, but it is too soon. It was only last night.*

Then the kiss was over, and she looked closely at him, but could see no sign that he was aware that she had withheld herself. After all, she had confessed that she did not love him yet, so he would not expect more.

He asked if she would mind if he spoke to Charlie now, and impulsively she took his hand led him forthwith into the dining room, where the rest of the family looked up at them in surprise.

"Charlie, Mr. Madd—Hampton," she amended hastily, "has something he would ask you."

And Hampton, stammering only slightly in his flusterment, told Charlie that Augusta had agreed to marry him if they had his permission.

This speech brought everyone around the couple with much kissing and crying and glad exclamations. Presently Hampton went away to go and tell his mother the happy news, after promising, at Mallory's pressing invitation, to come back and take dinner with them.

Sophia, still holding Augusta's hand, began pulling her to the stairs as soon as the door closed behind Hampton.

"I *must* hear all about it, darling Gussie, and I have something I must talk to you about. Please come up with me," she begged.

Mallory and Charles, their arms about each other, were going into Charlie's library, Mallory talking excitedly, so there was nothing for Augusta to do but settle down for a good long talk and exchange of confidences with Sophia, which Augusta thought she would not be able to bear at this moment. But so determined was Sophia that she had no choice.

However, Sophia succeeded in surprising her. After telling her again how happy she was about her dear Gussie and Hampton Madderson, she began on her own problems.

"Gussie, you will never believe what has happened to me, I can hardly believe it myself. I have fallen in love!" she pronounced in a tone mingling triumph and wonderment.

"Well, yes, Sophia," laughed Augusta, "hardly astounding news, dear one, since you have been engaged a fortnight."

"Oh, no, Gussie. I mean, it is not—oh dear, I can see that this is going to sound very strange. You see, it is Courtley I have fallen in love with!"

"Courtley! But—but—"

"Yes, I can see it *does* sound very strange, but let me

191

explain it to you, Gussie. You see, I think I must have always loved Courtley, but didn't know what it was, and then with Harry—well, it just sort of started and I was always very nervous, and I thought that was the way one was supposed to feel when one was in love. Oh, I know I must seem terribly stupid, but it was only ignorance, and surely I may be forgiven," she ended with a sort of breathless pleading.

"Of course, sweetheart, you may be forgiven by me," replied Augusta, still dazed by this revelation, "but it is Harry who must—"

"I know, I know, and that is why I am so anxious to speak to him. I cannot bear to think of how I must hurt him, but I cannot live with this falsehood between us. I hope he will think that I am but an inconstant ninny, and not some heartless flirt."

Augusta laughed at this appellation, for anyone less likely to be taken for a heartless flirt than Sophia she could not imagine.

"Soph, darling, you must, of course, speak to him as soon as possible and ask him to release you. I am sure he will be everything that is gentlemanly and kind, and it is, after all, the only thing you can in honor do."

"Exactly as I thought," said Sophia happily, "so I will tell him the very next time we are together. Oh, Gussie, is it not wonderful to be *in love?* I had no idea one could feel this way. I feel that I have grown wings and will fly at any moment. Do you feel that also?"

"Not exactly that," said Augusta evasively. "I think it takes people in different ways."

Blessedly, Sophia did not press Augusta on this point, but chattered on happily, telling her sister every tiniest detail of her discovery of love. Augusta smiled and nodded as though in agreement, and wondered desperately how she could contrive to be alone and pull her disordered thoughts together.

Although her heart leaped painfully when the maid tapped on the door to announce Lord Carnmoor below, Augusta felt an enormous relief to know that Sophia was leaving the room. She sat perfectly still, her eyes staring into space, and tried to make some sense out of Sophia's revelation.

Pointless to speculate on the course of events. If only Sophia had told her of this change in her feelings last night! Or if Harry had arrived before Hampton this morning. The fact was that Hampton had proposed, and she had accepted, and now Sophia was down below breaking her engagement to Harry. Senseless for Augusta's heart to cry out that now Harry was free. The fact remained that Augusta was not. She could not do such a terrible thing to Hampton as to ask for her release, after witnessing the happiness on his face when she accepted him. *How is it possible for so many good and well-meaning people to get themselves into such a terrible tangle,* she wondered hopelessly.

After barely twenty minutes behind the closed drawing-room door, a dazed-looking Harry emerged, followed by a contrite, but far from unhappy-looking, Sophia.

She had begun the moment she entered the room, and had continued her tale without stopping until she had confessed everything. Harry had hardly been prepared, when she did finish, to speak. To find that she did not love him, had apparently never loved him, but accepted him only because she thought she had led him on and was honor-bound to accept his proposal, was not news to be so easily assimilated. To realize that they had both been acting out a sort of ritual play, each thinking the other was the more involved, and neither being honest enough to examine his or her true feelings. *No,* he thought, *that is not quite true, for I did examine mine, but by then I felt it was too late, and that I could not hurt this sensitive creature.* The folly of all this wasted emotion was the main thought he carried out the door with him, after having assured Sophia that of course he released her from their engagement, and only wished her happy with Courtley.

As he walked off down the street, completely forgetting his patient groom standing ready to throw him up into the saddle of his equally patient horse, he told himself that if he had had as much courage as Sophia, he would have confessed his own feelings for Augusta. But he could not speak of it yet to anyone *but* Augusta. *How soon can I decently go to her,* he wondered.

som muchi, the poor man is much too nice everything. He
would have comradely-drawn feelings for Amanda. But he
could not see in either an amante; Buy even to marry
live-so... some am... to make them... I could ...

Chapter Twenty-two

Bramforth Wixton, slouching moodily on his spine before
his drawing-room fire, was ruminating on the unkindness
of Fate in his life. The Lord knew he had only the best
of intentions, and that he tried very hard to be everything
that was pleasing, but good fortune ever eluded him.

He had paid assiduous court to Augusta Portman,
shown her every consideration and paid her every compliment. Just think of that evening at Vauxhall, for example. They were out of pocket a pretty penny for that
evening alone. And for what? The girl had hardly let him
hold her hand and then had spent the rest of the evening
flirting with that damned Hastings.

And in the matter of the elopement, his intentions had
certainly been honorable. Could he help it that they
looked exactly alike, those girls? It was a mistake any
man could have made. There was no need for Coverly to
have said such derisory things when he heard of what had

happened. The thought of Bruce's cutting tone made Bramforth flinch, even now.

And hadn't he told the blasted girl he would take her back to London as soon as he had discovered his mistake? There was no need for her to go running off in that way and presenting a picture of persecution to Armstead, when the latter had caught them up. If she had only waited until Bramforth had had his luncheon, they would have been well on their way back long before Armstead reached the inn, and she would have been safely returned to her family and no one the wiser and no harm done.

Certainly it would have precluded the embarrassment he had suffered this morning in his club, when Charles Portman had cut him dead in front of everyone. Thinking on this humiliation, Bramforth was interrupted when the door burst open and his mother advanced, with great agitation, into the room.

"I have never been so mortified in my life, I vow. I cannot think what has come over Mrs. Portman to treat me so! Why, 'twas only day before yesterday that she was so kind and offered me a place in her carriage to go shopping, and now, this morning she won't receive me. Can you believe it, Bramforth?"

But Bramforth only hunched further down in the chair and made no comment.

"Bramforth, do you hear me? What can have come over Mrs. Portman to treat me so rudely? I know she was receiving, for I saw Beaumont going in as I came up the street. Can it be that she wanted to be alone with him?" This thrilling thought made her eyes shine for a moment, but then doubt clouded them. "Surely not, for never have I seen a more devoted couple than the Portmans. But then why did"—She broke off to stare suspiciously at Bramforth. "Have you said anything to Miss Portman that could have been taken amiss, Bramforth?"

"I've not even spoken to her for several days," replied Bramforth in an injured voice.

"Well, maybe *that* is the reason. Perhaps they were expecting more attention from a courting man. Why haven't you been there every day, as she has every right to expect if your intentions are serious?"

"Damned if I can be blamed——" burst out Bramforth.

"Bramforth! Please do not use that language in front of your mother."

"Well, I don't know what more I can be expected to do," continued Bram, hardly heeding her. "I could not even get her to go driving with me. She had so many engagements she——"

"Driving? What do you mean, driving? You have no carriage."

"Well, I had arranged to borrow one. And then all that money for hiring the horses, it's cost me a pretty penny, I can tell you."

"But if she would not go, why had you need to hire horses?"

But Bramforth, realizing how close he had come to confessing the whole thing, began backtracking in an effort to throw his mother off the scent. However, Mrs. Wixton, blind though she might be to his shortcomings, was well enough acquainted with her son to know when he was lying to her. Just as he had done when a small boy, his eyes, usually so sleepy and half-lidded, came wide open in a simulation of innocence, while his hands twisted together. Remorselessly she questioned him until she had the whole unsavory story from him. Though she had never fainted in her life, this recital caused her to turn pale and reach for her vinaigrette. Somewhat restored, she sat up and gave Bramforth such a tongue-lashing as made the remarks of his friend Bruce Coverly seem pale in comparison.

Bruce, meanwhile, had fared, if anything, even worse. Following Charles up the steps of White's, he had thought to retrieve some small scrap of pleasure out of the shattering of his brilliant plan to give the Portmans a set-down.

"Miss Sophia all recovered from her little escapade?" he inquired softly to Charles' back, with a significant snigger.

As Charles swung around his fist came with it, to land squarely on Bruce's nose. Bruce flew back down the steps to land sprawled on his backside on the pavement, blood spurting from his nose in every direction. He looked up in a daze of pain to see Charles calmly proceeding into the club without a backward glance, and all the windows lined with the grinning faces of every gentleman who counted for anything in London, who seemed to have chosen just that moment to be standing there waiting to witness his humiliation.

Chapter Twenty-three

Two days later, Mallory, returning from a shopping expedition, found Harry on the doorstep as she came up.

"Harry, how nice this is. Do come in with me and I will make you a cup of tea and we can have a chat."

"Thank you, Mallory, but the fact is—well, I have the carriage here, and I was going to see if Augusta would care for a drive," he said somewhat diffidently.

"Oh, she has gone with Hampton to—ride," she said, hastily changing her story when she realized that after all the news had not been publicly announced about Augusta's engagement, and that it was not her news to tell.

"I see. Well, then, I will take you up on your offer of tea," he said.

When they were settled across the tea table, Mallory began to tell him of how sorry she felt to know that Sophia had been the cause of any unhappiness for him, and of how much she and Charles admired him for the honorable way he had behaved in the circumstances.

"Well, while I am grateful to you both for your admiration, I must confess that it was not such a shattering blow as all that. In fact—"

"Yes?" She prodded him, for he had stopped and was staring off into space as though he had forgotten she was there.

"Oh. I beg your pardon. I fear I tend to do that these last few days. The fact is I was not as truthful with Sophia as she was with me. I was in love, also, you see, and I think I discovered it long before Sophia discovered her own true feelings."

"Harry! How awful for you! I mean, how wonderful. That is, it is wonderful now, if you see what I mean. I had been so worried, but this relieves my mind greatly. Oh, I can hardly wait to tell Charles. I know he will feel the same way about it. Our one concern was for you. Can you tell me who the fortunate girl is?"

"Augusta," he said simply.

Mallory was so startled that her cup jerked dangerously in its saucer, and she carefully set it back on the tray.

"Not . . . not . . . our Augusta?" she asked hopefully.

Harry, looking at her thunderstruck face, laughed lightheartedly, like a schoolboy without a care.

"Indeed it is *our* Augusta. *My* Augusta. Oh, Mallory, if you could know what I have gone through with this tangle, and now to be set free to—"

Mallory, unable to hear another word, reached across and put her hand over his mouth.

"Hush, please say no more, darling Harry. Oh dear, what shall I do? I must tell you—" But she stopped.

Harry looked at her queerly, knowing that a blow was coming. He reached up and took her hand away from his mouth.

"Go ahead, tell me, Mallory."

"My dear, she is engaged to Hampton Madderson."

"When—when did this happen?" he managed to choke out.

"That same morning that Sophia asked you to release her. In fact, not an hour before you came."

"I—see." Harry rose, and, taking Mallory's hand,

kissed it courteously with a bow. "You will forgive me if I rush away now, Mallory, and tell Charlie that I was sorry not to find him at home." He turned and walked stiffly from the room, not aware of what he had said or of how he got out onto the sidewalk. Again he walked off down the street, ignoring his puzzled coachman and groom, who had been waiting for him at the curb.

The duchess, dozing by the fire, heard the front door closing and footsteps going past the door to the stairs. Knowing it was Harry, she called to him, and heard the footsteps halt. After a moment he came into the room.

"Good God, Harry! What is it? You look all to pieces," exclaimed his mother.

Harry crossed to the sofa opposite her and slumped down heavily.

"Are you truly so cut up, Harry? I had thought you seemed rather relieved by the broken engagement than otherwise."

"Mama, did you have any suspicion that it was not Sophia here at the party on Wednesday?"

"Not Sophia? Why, what can you mean, Harry?"

"It was not Sophia. It was Augusta pretending to be Sophia. Shall I tell you how I found out? I kissed her. I knew immediately that it was Augusta. Don't ask me how. And though I knew I loved her already, I would have staked my life at that moment that she loved me also."

"Dear boy, please wait a moment," she pleaded. "Let me try to get this sorted out in my mind. *Why* would it have been Augusta pretending that night?"

"I don't know."

"Then can you tell me how you are so sure, other than the kiss, I mean? Did she tell you so, or did Sophia?"

"No. Sophia said nothing about it, and I assumed she did not want to embarrass Augusta by exposing the trick."

"All right. For some reason, on that night, Sophia did not come and Augusta came in her place, and carried it off very well, by the way. Now, if you knew this since that night, can you tell me why you are behaving this way today?"

"Because I found out today that she is engaged to Hampton Madderson."

The duchess thought about this for a moment and then finally figured out what he had been saying to her.

"Let me see if I have this straight," she said with great patience. "You realized that night when you kissed her, that it was Augusta you were kissing, because you were already in love with her and not Sophia. And you thought, from her response that night, that she felt the same way about you. And, no doubt, you went there today, hoping to confirm it and learned that she had entered into an engagement with Mr. Madderson?"

"Yes. That is precisely the case."

"Ah. Well, my dear boy, I wish with all my heart that it were not so, for I liked that girl very much and have always thought she would suit you better than Sophia. Though of course, I had no objections to Sophia. Sweet child."

The duchess said no more, though her heart was filled with a yearning to comfort her son. However, for this pain no mother's words would help, as well she knew. Nor indeed would anyone's words. This sort of pain must just be endured, with the knowledge that time alone could ease it.

The disintegration of the engagement between Sophia Portman and the Duke of Carnmoor created its own stir in London society, but like all such things it faded away as a source of gossip after a few days, to be replaced by the latest on dit concerning the possibility of Lord So-and-So forming an attachment for the eldest daughter of Lady Such-and-Such.

Mallory and Charlie, in spite of their feelings for Harry, could not help but rejoice for Courtley. One look at the radiant faces of Sophia and Courtley could make any heart lighter, and before naming a date for their wedding they awaited only a letter from old Lady Armstead, giving them her blessings.

Their joy only highlighted the fact that things were not good for Augusta. All her family watched with growing concern as she grew paler and yet more hectic. She threw herself into a frenzy of social activity, with an engagement for practically every hour of the day. And yet she was rarely seen doing more than toying with her food, and the dark circles under her eyes were testimony to sleepless nights. Mallory fretted more than ever, but could not persuade her to cease her endless round of picnics, soirées, dinners and balls.

Hampton himself was becoming alarmed about his fiancée. They went everywhere together, their announcement had been in the *Times,* Mrs. Madderson had been more than happy to welcome her as a future daughter-in-law, and all seemingly could not have been more happy for them. And yet he sensed all was not well with his beloved. The gnawing, secret worry for him was his fear that, far from engaging her affections as their relationship grew, he actually repulsed her to the point where she was regretting her decision. He tried, carefully, to question her about her feelings, always afraid to probe too far for fear of learning what he did not really want to hear.

Charles and Mallory both took their turns at trying to talk with Augusta, urging her to confide in them the source of her apparent unhappiness. But she only pooh-poohed their worries, telling them that she had never had a better time in her life, and was only enjoying the excitement of a newly engaged girl. But Sophia was unable to accept this explanation. Having found such perfect happiness herself, she could not believe that what her twin was experiencing was joy. She tackled Augusta with her doubts one night after Beth had finally left them in bed, with only the dying fire to light up the room. But though she wheedled and cajoled, she could not make Augusta confide in her. Finally Augusta turned away, saying she was weary and must sleep, leaving Sophia frustrated and unconvinced.

Several days later, her appearance at the breakfast table caused Mallory to gasp and rise to come around the table to feel her forehead. Augusta's cheeks flaunted two unnaturally bright spots of color, and her eyes were glassy in their dark circles, but she pushed Mallory's hand away in irritation.

"Please stop fussing, Mal. I am late this morning and must hurry if I'm to be dressed before Hampton arrives. We're to ride with the Holroyds this morning."

"Augusta, my darling, surely you should be in bed? I can see without even touching you that you are running a fever—" began Mallory.

Augusta sprang up with an exclamation. "Why does everyone persist in telling me that something is wrong with me! There is nothing *wrong!* I am very well and very happy!"

And with that she slipped very slowly to the floor in a dead faint in front of her aghast family.

Chapter Twenty-four

Since no amount of persuasion had been forceful enough to pry Sophia away from the bedside of her sister, it was Mallory who followed Dr. Crabshaw down the steps. Charles stopped pacing to stare questioningly at their solemn faces. From a bench against the wall, Hampton sprang up to join him.

"How is she?" Hampton asked before Charles could speak.

Dr. Crabshaw glared at them crossly from beneath his overhanging eyebrows. "Young women who go without eating for days on end and then dance the night away on top of all can hardly expect to enjoy the best of health!"

He took his hat from Williams, muttered, "Good day," and stomped out the door.

Both Charles and Hampton looked somewhat relieved at his pronouncement, but the look on Mallory's face did not match theirs.

"He may say what he likes, but it's my belief there is more than that to say to it. After all, she was unconscious for the better part of twenty minutes, and when she did come around she was talking wildly about—" She stopped abruptly. "Well, never mind about that, but I am very worried, I must confess. Dr. Crabshaw may say what he likes about exhaustion and not eating enough!"

"But what did the doctor do for her, Mal?" asked Charles.

"Oh, he gave her a sedative, and told me I must keep her in bed for at least a week and feed her only red beef and port wine to build up her blood. But it seems to me a strange prescription for someone running a fever."

"Well, at least he didn't bleed her, which is their usual remedy, no matter the malady."

"Oh, he suggested it, but I absolutely refused to allow it. Why, the child is white as a ghost as it is. I've my own way of bringing down a fever without the use of leeches, thank you," Mallory said, with a shiver of disgust.

"Where is Sophia?"

"She's bathing Augusta's face and arms. That is my way of bringing down the fever. Since Sophia refused to leave the room for a moment, I thought it best to give her something to keep her busy."

"Mrs. Portman, is there nothing I could do to help?" begged Hampton, whose face seemed almost haggard with worry.

Mallory patted his arm and assured him that everything was being done that could be done, but they would notify him immediately if there should be something he could help them with. He had to be satisfied with that and went away reluctantly.

Sophia, sponging the perspiration gently from Augusta's fevered brow, felt the tears welling up into her eyes at the sight of that still, pale face. The cheekbones stood up alarmingly and the eyes seemed sunk far back in their sockets. But mostly it was the sealed-off look of her sleeping face, so unattainable to help or comfort, that made Sophia's heart ache. Helplessly, she dropped the sponge in the basin and began her usual fruitless search for her handkerchief. She made a little sound, between a sob and a laugh and bent over to wipe her eyes on her hem, then, lifting one of Augusta's thin arms from beneath the coverlet, she began to sponge it with the cool water from the basin.

By afternoon, word of Miss Portman's illness had reached a great number of people and the calls began. No one, of course, asked to come into the house; that would have been ill-mannered. But all left their cards after inquiring kindly for news, and went away. There also came a large number of bouquets of flowers and baskets of fruit.

Mrs. Wixton, thinking to mend her fences while the family, she hoped, were in a weakened condition from worry about Augusta, had come hurrying around to offer her sympathy. She had learned from the duchess that Sophia and Harry were no longer engaged, but she had still to hear about Courtley Armstead. It seemed to her that it might be possible to present Bramforth in the light of a man hopelessly in love now with Sophia, after spending time in her company—no, no, better not to allude to that unfortunate incident at all unless the Portmans did, and then explain that Bramforth was a headstrong man driven by love, and such things as that. Surely they must be understanding of youth in the first flush of love?

However, no amount of her contrivings were to any avail in the stony, unyielding face of Williams. He was never discourteous, but he firmly refused her admittance, and finally she had to admit defeat and go away.

Of course, there were people who came every day and *were* admitted: Hampton, Courtley and Harry. All of them were received for the most part by Mallory, though occasionally Sophia could be persuaded to slip out of the sickroom to come down for a few moments with Courtley. But generally it was Mallory who had to deal with their worry.

Courtley began to fret, because on the few occasions when it was possible to have a word with Sophia, she looked pale and exhausted herself, and Mallory must needs reassure him that she saw to it that Sophia had enough rest, but that the poor child was naturally worried about her sister.

Harry, nearly frantic with anxiety for Augusta, had to limit his expression of it to gravely quiet inquiries, for never would he want the family, already guilty about the broken engagement with Sophia, to suffer more guilt over his unrequited love for Augusta. But he could not give up his daily visit to learn of her progress, and since he saw only Mallory and she already knew the state of his emotions, he felt it was not too much of a burden for them. The duchess came twice herself, but would not come in, staying only long enough to press Mallory's hand in sympathy, and express the hope that they would call upon her if anything at all was needed. Another time she came to bring a basket of grapes she had sent for from her own greenhouses at her country estate.

Hampton's visits were, for Mallory, the hardest ones of all. After the first few words explaining the state of Augusta's health at the moment, there was little else for them to say, yet Hampton could not leave. He would sit silently, obviously greatly perturbed, from time to time casting anguished, almost pleading, glances at Mallory. She tried her best to respond with soothing words, but was almost tongue-tied herself with the new knowledge she had carried about with her since the day of Augusta's collapse.

When Augusta had finally revived, she seemed to be in a delirious state, and while most of her ravings had been so incoherent as to be meaningless, Mallory had understood enough to have made the state of affairs suddenly clear. She could not know if Sophia had heard and understood, so great had been the agitation and activity of those moments. However, Mallory assumed that she had not, since Sophia had not spoken of it to her; poor Mallory didn't know who she felt the sorriest for, Hampton or Harry.

Sophia, though she had not spoken of it, had been just as attentive as Mallory to words muttered by her twin, and equally as quick to recognize the import of those words. Her own name, after all, had figured, largely coupled with Harry's. There was Hampton's name accompanied by much distressful tossing of the head on the pillow. But more heart-rending than all the rest was "Harry, my darling—too late—oh, what have I done?"

After all, thought Sophia, even the meanest intelligence could have no difficulty working out the reasons for Augusta's unusual behavior these past weeks after hearing *that*. Sophia had thought her heart would break when she heard that unhappy sighing speech, but had not mentioned it to Mallory, feeling that it was something she could only discuss with Augusta when Augusta was better.

Indeed, for all intents and purposes, Augusta *was* better. After the first day, when she had slept the whole time, mostly due to the laudanam administered by the doctor, she had been awake and aware and completely calm. But no one who saw her could say that she was actually recovered. She lay completely passive against her pillows, accepting without demur all administrations of hot gruel or medicaments. She spoke briefly of her own foolishness in accepting so many social engagements as to exhaust herself, and answered all queries with a pitiful attempt at cheerfulness, but other than that she simply lay there.

After a week of this, worn out with her self-imposed vigil and almost distracted with her worry for Augusta's unhappiness, Sophia chanced to come down the stairs just as Hampton was being admitted. He looked at her hopefully and came forward to take her hands before she could elude him.

"Sophia! I had so hoped to have a word with you. Please tell me, how is Augusta today? Is she better?" he asked, with such a pleading look in his haggard eyes that Sophia felt her heart turn over with pity for him.

"Oh, Hampton, my dear, she's—" Sophia tried to answer, but her throat tightened with tears and she could only cling to his hands speechlessly.

"Why, what is this, Sophia? Do you think she is worse? You must *tell* me. I beg you to tell me!"

"No, no, forgive me, Hampton, for alarming you. She is not worse, only—"

"Only not better? Is that it?"

She nodded and they stood there silently for a moment, Hampton staring fixedly ahead of him. Finally he sighed deeply and turned back to her again.

"Sophia, could I possibly impose upon you for a few moments' private conversation? I know you must be exhausted and have a thousand things to think of, but I would be most grateful. I promise not to take long."

"Of course, dear Hampton. Please come into Charlie's study. He has gone out for the morning, and I know we can be uninterrupted there."

However, once seated before the fire, with the door safely closed behind them, he seemed not to know how to begin. Finally, he gave her a wry little smile and spread his hands helplessly.

"I—now that I am here—it seems difficult to—I can't think how I can ask you what I had in mind to ask you without seming offensive. I know I have no right to ask you this, and you must just send me about my business if I—"

"Please, Hampton, do not distress yourself so much. Do you just speak what is in your heart and be assured that I will not take offense," she replied quietly, though her heart had begun to thump unpleasantly in anticipation of what she felt sure he was going to ask her.

"Well, it's just that, for some time now, I have felt— oh, I cannot say exactly what it is, for you must know with what joy I received Augusta's acceptance of my proposal. But it has been a kind of fearful joy at the same time. I suppose I must always have sensed that it would not come to be. Oh, I know that she did not feel for me as I felt for her, but I thought at the beginning that I could change her, make her love me. I have not been successful, but worse, I think I have been the cause for much unhappiness, unwitting on both our parts, of course, but true nevertheless. Sophia, has she said anything to you on this subject?"

Oh God, thought Sophia, *what can I say to this poor fellow after such a speech? It sounded as though he tore it out of himself and is still bleeding inside. I could truth-*

fully say "No," for indeed, she didn't say anything to me, and after all, have I the right to confirm his worst fears, based on what I heard from Augusta when she was out of her senses?

And yet, having heard it and being quite sure of its meaning, is it right to reassure him and thus prolong the suffering for both of them? Would Augusta thank me for interfering in what was, after all, her own business?

No, she thought regretfully, I cannot do it. I must speak to Augusta first.

"No, my dear, she has said nothing. But I promise I will speak to her and see if she will consent to a visit. I think it were best that you speak to her directly."

He pressed her hands and then raised them to kiss them warmly. "Thank you, my dear. Thank you very much. I will leave you now. I will call again tomorrow at this time, and if there is any word for me—"

"Of course, I will come down directly I hear you arrive. You may be sure of that."

She went back to Augusta's room, trying to think how best to present the problem to her. It was most daunting to see that wan, listless face sunk back into a pillow no whiter than her skin. Augusta raised tired eyelids, smiled fleetingly as Sophia came in, and then closed them again.

How to bring up such an emotional subject in the face of such lack of interest in anything? However, Sophia, with the image of Hampton's unhappy face in front of her, pulled the chair closer to the bedside and leaned forward to take the thin hand lying on the coverlet.

"Gussie, my darling, I must speak to you of something very serious, even though I know you are tired. I cannot watch you like this any longer, not when I think I know what the trouble is."

Augusta's eyes flew open at this statement and fastened on Sophia's face intently. It was the first sign of animation Augusta had shown for over a week, and it so startled Sophia she forgot what she was saying.

"Gussie! Why, darling, what—oh—yes, well, the truth is, Gussie, I just had a conversation with Hampton, and I think you should allow him to step up here to talk to you tomorrow."

The eyelids closed and the head turned away. "No, no, I am not up to visitors, Sophia."

"Gussie—Gussie, please look at me," Sophia begged, tugging on the hand she held. "I think you are not being fair to Hampton, nor to yourself—nor to—Harry." She said this last name with a gasp, determined to get it out, but frightened by the possible consequences. She felt the figure on the bed go completely still at that time. Good Heavens, had she caused a relapse? She stood up and leaned over to look more closely at the still face. Was she breathing?! But slowly the eyes opened, and two pairs of pansy-brown eyes confronted each other. Then slowly Augusta's filled with tears, and they ran unheeded down her cheeks.

"Oh, Gussie, my dearest one," cried Sophia, and she sat down on the bed and threw her arms about Gussie and wept with her. Finally, with a little laugh, she sat up to dry both their faces.

"There now, I have soaked your pillow, poor thing. Do raise your head, love, and I will turn the pillow so you will not be lying in the damp."

She made herself very busy with this to cover the embarrassment of the moment, and then sat back down on the bed.

"Soph, you know? How did you guess?" Augusta asked.

"My love, forgive me. I don't like to be interfering in your business, but it was something you said when you were out of your senses. Something about Harry." And Sophia told her of the words she had heard Augusta saying in her delirium. "And I think you must tell Hampton that it will not work and ask him to release you. I am sure he would not want to think he was making you so unhappy you fell ill from it."

"Oh, Sophia, *how* can I do such a thing? He is so good, so kind to me always, and I feel such regard for him. I would not hurt him for anything in the world."

"I think it will do far more hurt to him to marry him

when you love another. I mean, if you did not love someone else, it would be different, but since you do, it is not fair not to tell him of it. As you told me yourself it—it's the only honorable thing to do, Gussie," she ended stoutly.

"I know you are right, dear heart, but my heart fails me when I think of such an interview."

"I will—" Sophia began reluctantly.

"No, my darling, I know what you are going to offer, and if I didn't know already, it would be proof positive that you love me for you to make such an offer. But it is something I must do myself. Tomorrow I will get up and dress. I will not have him find me a pitiful, begging creature in bed."

"Darling, I'm sure Mallory would not allow—"

"I'll sit on the chaise then, but I will dress."

"Well, I should think that wouldn't be harmful, and I know you will feel much better once it has been said, Gussie. I know I felt much better as soon as I was straight with Harry."

"You know, Soph, I think on the whole your adventure was very good for you, aside from the obvious way, I mean, of discovering your love for Courtley. You have become more courageous."

"Guss, now you are flattering me," laughed Sophia. "I fear I will never have a very brave heart."

"And I suppose it was not a brave heart that escaped from Bramforth and hid in the tree, and faced Harry and—"

"Oh, no, my love. I but tried to imagine what *you* would do in such situations and pretended to be you!"

Chapter Twenty-five

Augusta gave Hampton, who was advancing toward her across the room, her bravest smile, hoping that the morning light did not reveal too drastically the sad thinness of her face. Beth had spent a full hour brushing and arranging Augusta's hair, and had applied the faintest film of rouge on each cheek, so that Augusta felt she did not look too pale. Augusta had been determined not to in any way make Hampton feel sorry for her. She had made a most unhappy decision and must now remedy it. She felt that no matter how difficult it would be for her to admit it, it could not be nearly so hard on her as it would be for him to have to hear it, so she must face it bravely without flinching.

He took her hand and kissed it lingeringly, then with his finger, tilted her face up to him and looked at her closely.

"Well, my dear, you have given us all a great fright, but we will forgive you for it if you will but promise that you will recover quickly," he said, smiling gently at her.

"Hampton, my dear, you are too kind, as always. All the lovely flowers every day—"

He waved this away and turned to pull forward a chair for himself.

"Now, my sweet Augusta, I must speak to you very seriously."

"And so must I speak to you. I have had some days now, with nothing to do but lie here and think upon my sins and I—"

"Augusta?" He interrupted her firmly. "Ordinarily I would not dream of interrupting a lady, nor would I insist that what I have to say is so important that it must be heard first, but this once I must insist. I too have been given most seriously to think this past week. I love you. I think you know that. But I fear we have rushed into something without enough thought. I believe we must, both of us, agree that it has all been too hastily done, and release each other from our promises for now. Perhaps, after some time has passed we will both want to think of marriage again and can then—"

Augusta held out her hands to him pleadingly, and he took them. She swallowed desperately, willing herself not to cry. In spite of all her resolve this morning to face him without asking for anything, he had nearly broken her with this brave speech. She knew that he had worked out for himself the resistance of her heart to what her head had told her it would be good for her to do. Rather than give her pain, he had taken the blame upon himself, and also the burden of asking her to release him, rather than wait for her to be forced to do so.

"Yes, my dear, I can see you recognize the wisdom of what I say," he said, continuing as though she had spoken words of agreement, and patting her hands comfortingly. "These things are difficult, but we are two very sensible people who know how to deal with these matters in a sensible way. I discussed it with my mother last night, and she agrees with me that it will be the best thing for both of us. Now I need only to know that you will forgive me."

"I forgive you? Hampton, my dear, how can you say that, when I know you understand perfectly well that I—"

"There, I knew you would, with your great heart. We will be friends, will we not, as we have always been?"

"Yes." She answered faintly, hardly daring to trust herself to speak for fear she would burst into tears.

"Then I shan't tire you for another moment, my dear. I'm sure you should be back in your bed. I'll just go down and have a word with Charles, and you may be sure everything will be taken care of. You are to devote yourself to recovery, do you hear me?"

She reached up her hand to touch his face and then pulled down his head to kiss him very softly. "Thank you, dear Hampton, for everything, and I will say it, whether you will have me do so or not. I am more sorry than I can say that this has happened. I can only hope that you will forgive me."

He kissed each of her hands, smiled, and was gone. And now, finally, she allowed herself tears, and then she began sobbing and felt that she would not ever be able to stop. Sophia came in and held her while she cried, and then Mallory came and insisted that she get back into her bed immediately. Augusta was happy to obey, for she felt more tired than ever. She sank gratefully into the safety of her bed and closed her eyes and was asleep almost before Mallory and her sister had pulled the drapes and tiptoed out of the room.

The next afternoon, the duchess, nodding graciously to an acquaintance here and there, bowled along smoothly in her open landau and wondered if she would get the headache from the prattling voice next to her, and wondered yet again why she had always to obey her conscience when it came to Amabel Wixton. That woman set her teeth on edge with her constant chatter, and yet each time she thought of going out in her carriage, she felt compelled to offer to take Amabel with her. *Why cannot one's conscience leave one in peace when one reaches my age?* she thought. Mrs. Wixton was at this moment holding forth on the subject of Lady Egreton's gown. She thought it vastly unbecoming in a woman of four and thirty and the mother of six children to wear such a sheer gown, and in pink, of all colors, for all the world as though she were the veriest maiden fresh from the schoolroom.

"And I will stake my life she is *enceinte* again. No one can fool me about these things. Really, quite disgraceful with such a brood as she has already, four of them girls, too, and how she's to provide dowries for all of them, I shall never know. And that second son, my dear duchess, well, far be it from me to say anything, but everyone said there was something strange about that whole affair, what with her husband away in the Peninsula for so long, and besides, one has but to look at the boy to see he's the spit of the Earl of—"

She became aware that the duchess had raised her lorgnette and was staring at her with a very cold eye, and her voice stopped abruptly.

"Amabel, I think you forget yourself," the duchess reproved in frigid tones.

"I'm sure I meant no harm, my dear duch—" But the duchess had turned away to greet two gentlemen riders approaching the carriage.

"Mr. Madderson and Lord Hastings! How very nice." The duchess ordered the carriage to stop and held out her hand to them. They dismounted and came up to kiss it.

"My dear lady, this is enchanting. You are in especially good looks today, I see," said Hastings gaily, as the duchess smiled fondly upon him. He turned to bow to Mrs. Wixton. "Mrs. Wixton, good day. Are you ladies enjoying the sunshine?"

Mrs. Wixton simpered at him and asked playfully if they were to have two such handsome couriers for their drive.

"Alas, I am devasted not to be able to offer my services, but I am even now late for an engagement," said Hastings.

The duchess turned to Mr. Madderson. "And you, sir, must be on your way to the Portmans'. Tell me, what is the news of Miss Portman? I have heard that she was much better this morning. I could not go around myself, but sent my man around to inquire."

"She is better today indeed, Your Grace. I have just come from there myself and spoke to Mrs. Portman who told me so."

"Ah, these young girls, they *will* overdo during the Season. Well, now I suppose we must be hearing of a date for your nuptials very soon, sir."

"Madame, Miss Portman and I have mutually agreed that we will retract our announcement," he replied gravely, but firmly.

"My dear Mr. Madderson, I am sorry indeed to hear that," replied the duchess with all sincerity, in spite of the fact that her mind leaped instantly to Harry. She saw that the two gentlemen were staring past her, and that both of them were having some difficulty to keep from laughing, even Mr. Madderson, in spite of the sad pronouncement he had just made. She turned to find that Amabel Wixton was the cause of their amusement.

Mrs. Wixton, whose eyes and mouth had both opened wide in amazement at the news she had just heard, had apparently forgotten them, for they remained fixed open, while the intelligence that had caused them to behave in such a fashion swirled about in her brain, trying to find a point of advantage to herself in it.

"Amabel!" The duchess raised her lorgnette again, usually a deadly weapon against Mrs. Wixton, but this time she did not see it. "Amabel! What on earth's the matter with you? Why are you all agape like that? Amabel!"

The duchess rapped Mrs. Wixton sharply on the hand with her lorgnette, and Mrs. Wixton jerked back to an awareness of her surroundings.

"What? Oh. I beg your pardon—I just thought of something I forgot to do before setting out," she explained in some confusion. But though she adjusted her features, it was clear that she was more than a little abstracted for the rest of the drive. Finally the duchess ordered her coachman to drive Mrs. Wixton home.

Really, the duchess thought, *what an exasperating*

woman. What can have come over her to behave in such a ridiculous way?

Mrs. Wixton rushed into her drawing room in search of her son.

"Bramforth," she exclaimed breathlessly, "you will never believe what I have just learned."

"Probably not," he returned lazily.

"Sit up, do. I wish you will not always be slouching about like that. Now, what do you think? Augusta Portman and Mr. Madderson have broken their engagement!"

"Well, I can't see why you should be in such a taking about it. It's nothing to do with you," he retorted.

"Bramforth! Think what this could mean! This is your chance, my son. They will have quarreled and she will be unhappy and looking for some way to show him that she doesn't care, and you could snap her up with no trouble at all. Don't you see? Now is the time for you to act!"

"Be damned to that," he said, glowering up at her from under his brows, "I've had all the encounters I care to have with that family. They may all remain old maids for all I care. I'll have none of it."

"Bramforth, do you listen to your mother. You know I always know what is best for you. You know perfectly well—"

Bramforth's eyes slowly closed, and he allowed the sound of his mother's voice to become a background hum as he drifted off to sleep.

The duchess was in somewhat of a hurry to reach home herself, though whether she would impart her news to Harry or not she had not decided. As she descended from the carriage, she saw him just coming down the steps.

"Well, my boy, are you off somewhere? I see that we are forever missing each other these days," she said agreeably as they met on the pavement.

"I had thought to step around to the Portmans' to inquire of Augusta."

"Very nice. I sent 'round to inquire this morning and heard that she was much improved, and have but now met Mr. Madderson in the Park, who tells me the same thing."

"Yes? Well, Mama, I won't keep you standing on the pavement. Let me help you up the steps, and then I'll be on my way." He offered her his arm and took her to the door, then kissed her cheek and started back down.

The duchess hesitated, but then could not help herself, she felt compelled to tell him what she had heard, if only to see that heaviness disappear from his eyes for a moment.

"Harry, he told me they have broken their engagement."

He spun around and stood there for a moment, staring at her in astonishment. Then he cried, "Aha," and turned, and went running off down the street, while she stood there smiling after him, feeling almost giddy with pleasure.

"Just like his father," she murmured with satisfaction, and turned to the door.

When Williams opened the door to Harry, Sophia was just crossing the hall on her way upstairs.

"Why, Harry, good afternoon. You've come to inquire of Augusta, and I'm happy to tell you that she is very much better today."

Mallory and Charles came out of the library at this moment and greeted Harry warmly.

"Mallory, Charlie, lovely to see you, but if you won't think me rude, I won't stay to talk now. I must go up to see Augusta."

With a soft shriek Sophie ran to block his way on the staircase.

"Harry, you can't go up. Why, Gussie is in her wrapper, and Beth is brushing her hair. She can't see you now."

"Ah, but I must see her instantly," he said with a smile.

"I'll—I'll just go tell her you are here and—"

Harry took her by the waist and swung her about to set her down behind him. "No, my dear Sophia, I dare not wait even a moment. The last time I waited and was too late. Just think, she may even now be preparing to accept another proposal. You must see that I can't risk it." And with a laugh he turned and taking the stairs two at a time, disappeared from view.

Sophia watched him in astonishment, then turned to Mallory and Charles. They looked at each other for a moment, and then suddenly all began laughing at once.

Augusta, her hair down her back, was sitting at her dressing table while Beth administered the hair brush to the long golden curls. They had chosen a pale pink gown, and it was waiting, spread upon the bed, for Augusta was determined to go down to dinner.

They both looked up in amazement as the door burst open and Harry stood there.

"Harry!"

"Your Grace, what are you doing? You can't come in here," scolded Beth, recovering from her first shock and rushing toward him, hairbrush in hand, as though she would use it as a weapon to defend her mistress.

But Harry only laughed, shooed her out the door, and closed it behind her.

Augusta sat still at her dressing table, her heart seemed to have stopped abruptly at his entrance, and then as the door closed behind Beth and he stood there looking at her with a slight smile, it began again with a painful, slow thumping.

"Well, my dear," he said finally. "I think we have some things we must talk about."

"Do we, Harry?" she managed to say, trying not to display her agitation.

"Yes, very definitely," he replied and then stood there as though waiting for her to begin.

She studied his face trying to get a clue to what he was thinking. "I dislike appearing stupid, Harry, but fear I don't quite understand—"

"Do you not, my dear? Surely if you but think for moment, it will come to you that there is something you have to tell me." And again he smiled that strange smile.

And then she *did* know! He was waiting for her

explain about her deception the night of the duchess' party for Sophia. *Oh God,* she thought, *that seems so long ago now that I had completely forgotten about it.* And she felt also great embarrassment at what she had done to the duchess, not to speak of that passionate kiss they had exchanged when he had thought he was kissing Sophia! How explain her conduct then? Though he must have guessed to be questioning her.

"Harry, I do have something that I must explain to you. I'm afraid I have behaved very badly to you and your mother. The night of your dinner party for Sophia—it was I who came that night."

"Yes, I know."

"You *do* know! Then—how—I mean why did you not expose me? Does your mother know?"

"Yes, I told her. She said there must have been some very good reason for the deception."

Augusta then told him what the very good reason had been, and he looked grimly angry when he heard what Bramforth had done. But then his face lightened, when he realized that the outcome of Bramforth's terrible deed had been his release from his engagement from Sophia.

"It was all my idea," Augusta continued, "though Mallory was horrified that I should even suggest such a thing. However, we were all in such an upset, we none of us could think how best to solve the situation, and at that time could only think of protecting Sophia's reputation."

"Dear Augusta, I can only admire your ingenuity and my mother admires your acting talent. My real concern was that you tell me of it, so there would be no more deception between us."

And with these words he abandoned his position on the other side of the room and advanced toward her quickly, and with no hesitation at all he lifted her from the chair and held her crushed against him.

"Now, answer me straight. Have you seen any gentlemen since Hampton left here yesterday?"

"No, Harry," she said meekly.

"Then you've had no proposals since then?"

"No, Harry."

"You will marry me?"

"Yes, Harry."

There seemed to be no further need for conversation after that, so he kissed her—at length.